Valentine Bride

Holiday Brides, Book 1
A Sweet Western Romance
by
USA Today Bestselling Author
SHANNA HATFIELD

Valentine Bride
Holiday Brides Book 1

Copyright © 2016 by Shanna Hatfield
All rights reserved.

ISBN: 978-1523604173

All rights reserved. By purchasing this publication through an authorized outlet, you have been granted the nonexclusive, nontransferable right to access and read the text of this book. No part of this publication may be reproduced, distributed, downloaded, decompiled, reverse engineered, transmitted, or stored in or introduced into any information storage and retrieval system, in any form or by any means, including photocopying, recording, or other electronic or mechanical methods, now known or hereafter invented, without the written permission of the author, except in the case of brief quotations embodied in reviews and certain other noncommercial uses permitted by copyright law. Please purchase only authorized editions.

For permission requests, please contact the author, with a subject line of "permission request" at the e-mail address below or through her website.
shanna@shannahatfield.com

This is a work of fiction. Names, characters, businesses, places, events, and incidents either are the product of the author's imagination or are used in a fictitious manner. Any resemblance to actual persons, living or dead, business establishments, or actual events is purely coincidental.

Published by Wholesome Hearts Publishing, LLC.
wholesomeheartspublishing@gmail.com

To the elderly who live life to the fullest…

Books by Shanna Hatfield

FICTION

CONTEMPORARY

Holiday Brides
Valentine Bride
Summer Bride
Easter Bride
Lilac Bride
Lake Bride

Rodeo Romance
The Christmas Cowboy
Wrestlin' Christmas
Capturing Christmas
Barreling Through Christmas
Chasing Christmas
Racing Christmas
Keeping Christmas
Roping Christmas
Remembering Christmas

Grass Valley Cowboys
The Cowboy's Christmas Plan
The Cowboy's Spring Romance
The Cowboy's Summer Love
The Cowboy's Autumn Fall
The Cowboy's New Heart
The Cowboy's Last Goodbye

Summer Creek
Catching the Cowboy
Rescuing the Rancher
Protecting the Princess
Distracting the Deputy

Women of Tenacity
Heart of Clay
Heart of Hope
Heart of Love

HISTORICAL

Pendleton Petticoats
Dacey   Lacey
Aundy   Bertie
Caterina   Millie
Ilsa   Dally
Marnie   Quinn
*   Evie*

Pendleton Promises
Sadie

Baker City Brides
Tad's Treasure
Crumpets and Cowpies
Thimbles and Thistles
Corsets and Cuffs
Bobbins and Boots
Lightning and Lawmen
Dumplings and Dynamite

Hearts of the War
Garden of Her Heart
Home of Her Heart
Dream of Her Heart

Hardman Holidays
The Christmas Bargain
The Christmas Token
The Christmas Calamity
The Christmas Vow
The Christmas Quandary
The Christmas Confection
The Christmas Melody
The Christmas Ring
The Christmas Wish

Chapter One

"She's what?" Fynlee Dale screeched into the phone then glanced around as everyone in the office turned to stare at her.

Quickly dropping her voice to a normal level, she apologized to the bearer of such disturbing news. "I'm sorry, Sage. Are you… are you sure?"

When the caller repeated the statement, Fynlee rolled her eyes and rose to her feet. "I'll be right there."

Frantic to leave, she hung up the phone, turned off her computer, and stuffed the files she'd been working on into her desk drawer.

After grabbing her purse, she stopped by her supervisor's desk. Even though the two girls had been good friends since the sixth grade, at work they maintained a professional relationship. "I'm sorry, Carrie. I hate to ask, but…"

The woman offered her a sympathetic smile.

"Don't worry about it, Fynlee. Might I assume your grandmother is up to her old tricks?"

"As a matter of fact, this is a new one, but yeah, Grams is at it again."

Carrie glanced at the clock. "It's nearly quitting time for you anyway. Don't worry about leaving a little early."

"Thanks, Carrie. I appreciate it." Fynlee smiled at her friend then hastened out the door of the medical billing office where she worked.

Summer heat threatened to suffocate her when she stepped outside into the July afternoon.

She fumbled in her purse for her sunglasses and slid them up her nose as she rushed across the parking lot to her car. The hulking form of the hospital cast shadows over the employee parking area. The shade provided by the building kept her car from feeling like the inside of an oven when she opened the door.

Although it was a typical summer day in her Eastern Oregon town of Holiday, it didn't mean she appreciated the triple-digit temperatures. Not only did her fair skin blossom with freckles in the sun, it also burned with alarming speed.

In a rush to reach Golden Skies Retirement Village where her grandmother lived, Fynlee didn't take time to let the inside of her car cool before she drove out of the parking lot and down the street.

Grateful the retirement facility was less than a mile from the hospital, the location made it convenient for her to stop and visit her grandmother every day on her way home from work. Or to rush over when one of the staff called, in need of help handling her sometimes bizarre Grams.

Matilda Dorian Dale had never been what one would call classic grandmother material.

Words that best described the woman often included eccentric, unusual, and downright weird.

A few people at Golden Skies thought her grandmother was nuts, but the truth was that she was no more wacky than she'd ever been.

Grams and Gramps had raised Fynlee from the time she was eight. Over the years, she'd grown accustomed to her grandmother's strange ways. Nonetheless, Matilda had crossed a line today.

Dreading what she'd find inside the retirement center, Fynlee parked her car in the visitor area. She snagged her purse and a sack of magazines she promised she'd bring Grams then hurried inside.

The receptionist tipped her head toward the library located across the entry foyer when Fynlee stopped at her desk.

"She's in there?" Fynlee asked, setting her sunglasses on top of her head and dropping her car keys into her purse.

"She sure is." The receptionist, a kind young woman named Sage, nodded with a hint of sympathy.

"She's not really…" Fynlee couldn't bring herself to say the words. The picture created in her mind from merely thinking them was profusely troubling.

Unable to hide her smile, Sage's amusement sparkled in her eyes. "Yep, she is. Wait until you see her."

Fynlee took a deep breath and rolled her

shoulders back before entering the library. Only a few people were inside, all quietly reading books. As her gaze swept around the room, she vainly hoped Sage's report about her grandmother's latest quirk turned out to be incorrect. However, Sage was always honest and forthcoming, so there was no reason to doubt what she'd reported over the phone.

A sigh rolled out of her when Fynlee spied Matilda standing over a table, studying a large map of the world.

Nope.

Sage's report was absolutely, unerringly true.

Haste drove her across the room to her grandmother's side. The woman looked up at her with an affectionate smile.

"Fynlee, sweetie! What are you doing here?" Matilda's loud voice bounced off the walls. She embraced Fynlee, delivering a tight squeeze. "I didn't expect you for another hour."

The other occupants of the room looked up from their books with disapproving frowns. "Shh!"

Matilda scowled at them as Fynlee led her into the foyer and down the hallway to the elevator.

"Is everything okay, dear? Why are you here?" Matilda asked. She draped an arm around Fynlee's waist as they stepped off the elevator on the third floor and made their way to her apartment.

"I'm here, Grams, because I received a call about your interesting choice of attire this afternoon. Apparently, you decided to change things up after lunch today." Fynlee could barely restrain her laughter as her grandmother sashayed down the hall wearing a pair of her grandfather's old white briefs over black leggings. The tails of a billowing blouse, adorned with bright pink and yellow flowers on a black background, dangled through the legs of the tighty whities.

"It's positively ludicrous of them to call you." Matilda stopped in front of her door and looked at Fynlee. "I spilled soup on my slacks and needed to change. There's no law that says old women my age can't wear leggings."

"No, there isn't," Fynlee agreed. Her eyes widened when Matilda reached into the front of the briefs and pulled out her apartment key. Shocked, she swallowed the gum she'd been chewing.

Matilda whacked her on the back a few times, as she coughed and spluttered. Quickly, the older woman opened the door and pulled Fynlee inside.

"You need a drink of water, honey." Matilda hurried into her kitchen and returned with a glass of cold water.

Fynlee gulped it down as she toed the door shut, tamping down the urge to stamp her foot in frustration. Over the years, she'd seen her grandmother do any number of outlandish things, but this had to be near the top of the list.

"What on earth possessed you to wear Gramps' underpants today?" Fynlee had no idea where Grams had even found them. She thought she'd gotten rid of all but a few shirts and one coat that belonged to her grandfather before Grams moved into Golden Skies. Obviously, her grandmother had squirreled away more of his belongings than Fynlee suspected.

Gramps had been gone almost four years. Out

of the blue, about a year after his death, Grams declared it was time to sell the house they'd moved into as newlyweds. She announced she wanted to move to Golden Skies.

In the time Matilda had lived at the retirement village, Fynlee had received countless phone calls about her grandmother. Most of the staff knew Matilda Dale was harmless and sane, for the most part, despite her distinctive way of dancing through life.

However, some days the old gal seemed determined to tip the scales toward being ready for a room made of rubber.

If the odd behavior had been a recent development, Fynlee might have been concerned. Since her grandmother had always been that way, she wasn't worried.

Embarrassed — a little.

Amused — most definitely.

But not worried.

"Oh, you brought my magazines," Matilda said, taking the bag from Fynlee and setting it on her coffee table. She plopped down on the couch and perused the selections.

Fynlee took a seat beside her and tamped down her impatience. "Grams, why are you wearing those underpants?"

Matilda glanced down, as though she just realized what she wore. "My leggings don't have any pockets." The woman continued looking through the magazines and chose one, settling back against the vibrant orange and sunny yellow cushions scattered across her cobalt blue couch.

"Your leggings don't have pockets, so…?" Fynlee tried to rationalize why her grandmother connected that to wearing men's briefs.

"Well, this," Matilda tugged on the front of the briefs, "makes a wonderful place to carry things. It will hold my key, a little cash, and my lipstick. You know, darling, I never go anywhere without my lipstick."

Fynlee stared at her grandmother. She ought to be astounded by such absurd reasoning. Instead, she bit her cheek to keep from smiling. Matilda had a point, even if it was way, way out there, lingering on the border of crazy town.

"Grams, you can't go around wearing men's underpants, any underpants, on the outside of your clothes. And you really, really can't wear men's underpants at all." Fynlee gave her grandmother a cautionary glance. "Promise you won't wear them again."

"Now, honey, would I do such a thing?"

Fynlee laughed. "Yes, you would. I'm going to need a solemn promise."

Matilda got to her feet and strolled over to the window, staring down at the parking lot.

Suddenly, she squealed and clapped her hands like a thirteen-year-old at their first concert. "Oh, she's here, sweetie! She's here!"

"Who's here, Grams?" Fynlee stood and stepped over to the window, looking down at an elegant woman wearing a white straw hat with a pale blue cotton dress. Images of a southern belle floated through her mind, making her smile.

"It's Ruth. She called yesterday to let me know

she'd be moving in today. Did I tell you that?"

Fynlee shook her head, wondering how her grandmother failed to mention that important detail. The two women had been best friends for what seemed like forever.

Matilda clapped her hands again. "Her nephew bought the ranch a few months ago. I think you knew that."

At Fynlee's nod, she continued. "Anyway, Ruth stayed there until he got the hang of things."

Fynlee seriously doubted someone capable of taking over the Flying B Ranch needed advice from an octogenarian, particularly one who preferred to stay indoors and bake than work outside.

Over the years, Fynlee had visited the ranch on numerous occasions. The last time she took Matilda out there, Ruth had mentioned a relative purchased the place and would soon arrive to sign the papers. She'd sounded relieved to turn over responsibility for the sprawling acres and large farmhouse to her nephew.

Rather than listen to the conversation that ensued about the buyer, Fynlee had been more interested in watching the spring calves outside.

Although she hadn't seen Ruth since that visit a few months ago, Fynlee knew her grandmother frequently spoke with the woman. They had been friends for decades and when their husbands were alive, the two couples often enjoyed going to dinner or playing cards together.

Sometimes, Fynlee had been included in their plans, especially when it came to spending time at the ranch. A number of her fondest childhood memories came from riding horses at the Flying B and sledding down the hill behind the barn.

"We need to go downstairs and make Ruthie feel welcome," Grams said, starting for the door.

"Oh, no you don't, Miss Matilda." Fynlee caught her grandmother's hand in hers before she made it to the door. "If you want to leave this room, you are taking off those underpants and surrendering any other pairs you've been hiding."

For a long moment, Matilda glared at Fynlee in a battle of wills.

Fynlee raised one eyebrow, questioning how much Matilda wanted to see her friend.

In a huff, Matilda jerked off the briefs and tossed them at the coffee table. Without another word, she stomped into her bedroom. The sounds of her rummaging through a drawer and muttering to herself floated back to the living room.

She returned carrying half a dozen pairs of briefs. "Here," she said, handing them to Fynlee.

Before the woman changed her mind, Fynlee grabbed the pair off the coffee table and rolled her eyes when two quarters fell out. She unearthed a tube of lipstick, a wadded-up tissue, a five-dollar bill, and a slip of paper with a phone number.

"Whose number is this, Grams?" Fynlee held out the paper.

Matilda took the small piece of paper and set it on the desk near her phone. "That's Ruth's new number here. I don't want to lose that until I have it memorized." Before Fynlee could stuff the underwear into a bag or set down the contents of the improvised pocket, Matilda yanked on her arm and pulled her into the hall.

"Come on, honey. I want to say hello." Matilda marched down the hall with a death grip on Fynlee's arm. They reached the elevator at the same moment it opened and a handsome cowboy stepped out, cupping Ruth's elbow in his big hand.

Matilda released an ear-splitting squeal and wrapped her arms around Ruth while Fynlee and the man mutely observed.

"Gracious, Tillie, that is the most enthusiastic welcome I do believe I've ever received," Ruth said. Kindly smiling, she stepped back and adjusted the straw hat Matilda had knocked askew.

Ruth's voice always reminded Fynlee of warm honey, soothing and pleasant with a hint of sweetness.

"I'm so happy you're finally moving in Ruthie. We are going to have the best adventures now that you're here." Matilda looped her arm around Ruth's and the two of them sauntered to an apartment located down the hall.

Fynlee held back a sigh as she watched the older women, wondering how many calls from the staff loomed in her immediate future. Matilda got into enough mischief on her own, but now she'd be dragging poor Mrs. Beaumont into the fray.

A clearing throat drew her gaze to the brawny man standing beside her, staring at the underwear she held.

"Is that a welcoming gift?" he asked with a lopsided smirk.

Heat flamed into Fynlee's cheeks, making her freckles stand out even more as she hastily looked for somewhere to dump the briefs. With nothing readily available, she wadded them into a lumpy ball and clutched them against her side.

"No, it certainly is not. I don't think anyone would want these old things, anyway." Humiliated, she studied the burly, unreasonably attractive stranger. At her five-ten height, it wasn't often she encountered a man tall enough to make her look up to fully see his face.

A tanned forefinger tipped back the brim of his straw Stetson and Fynlee swallowed hard. Blue eyes sparkled with humor behind thick lashes and a boyish smile added to his considerable appeal. Hints of golden-brown hair peeked out from beneath the hat brim.

"I'm Carson Ford. Aunt Ruth asked me to help her get settled." He held out a work-roughened hand to her.

Fynlee glanced at it, noting a cut across the back of his knuckles and a jagged scar near his thumb. Those hands looked every bit as rugged as the man to which they belonged.

With only a slight hesitation, she reached out and shook his hand, unprepared for the electrical current that sizzled from her fingertips up her arm.

From the way Ruth spoke of her nephew who purchased the ranch, Fynlee assumed he'd be in his fifties. A picture of a pot-bellied, balding man had fit her image of him. She certainly never envisioned the nephew as a young, incredibly attractive cowboy.

Gathering her rapidly scattering wits, she smiled at him. "It's nice to meet you, Mr. Ford. I'm

Fynlee Dale. That loony woman with your aunt is my grandmother."

The sound of his deep chuckle made something softly pluck at her heartstrings. For a brief, fleeting moment, Fynlee toyed with the idea that she'd finally met the man she would one day marry.

Stunned by the preposterous notions swirling through her mind, she took a step back and turned toward her grandmother's apartment. In her twenty-seven years of living, she'd never seen a man as virile and entirely appealing as Ruth's nephew, but that was no reason to lose her head.

"I've met your grandmother before. In fact, I recall seeing her several times at the ranch when I was younger," Carson said, keeping step with her as they walked down the hall. "She's a lively woman, that's for sure."

"Lively?" Fynlee stopped outside Matilda's door. "That's a very nice way of putting it, Mr. Ford."

"It's Carson, ma'am." He smiled and his blue eyes twinkled with mirth. "I think your grandmother is good for my aunt."

Delighted by his words and his engaging presence, Fynlee opened Gram's door then turned back to him. "Call me Fynlee. I sincerely hope some of your aunt's calm gentility rubs off on Grams, but I'm not holding my breath."

Carson chuckled again and tipped his hat to her before moving down the hall to his aunt's apartment.

Fynlee watched him walk away with a slight swagger in the gait that carried his well-built form.

Dreamily, she stepped inside her grandmother's apartment and realized she still held an armful of her grandfather's old underpants.

If that hadn't sent Carson Ford running for the nearest exit, perhaps she'd see him around again.

Chapter Two

Carson Ford smiled as he tightened the cinch on his saddle. Every time he recalled meeting Matilda Dale's granddaughter, it made him want to laugh.

The mortified look on her face as she stood in the hallway with an armful of men's underwear made him wonder what she and her grandmother were up to before he and Aunt Ruth arrived. Her cheeks were nearly as red as the berry-red blouse she'd worn.

In the week since he'd settled his aunt at Golden Skies, Carson often found his thoughts lingering on the tall, dark-haired enchanting Fynlee Dale.

Beautiful hazel eyes, fair skin, and a healthy sprinkling of freckles gave her a wholesome, fun appearance. Kindness radiated from her, especially in the way she lovingly attended to her grandmother and his aunt.

If he'd ever had a sister, Carson would have wanted her to be just like Fynlee, or at least like the picture of her he'd painted in his imagination.

Despite his mother's longing for a daughter, it wasn't meant to be. His parents decided they'd end up with a house full of rascally boys instead of the precious princess Evie Ford so badly wanted if they continued having children. Wisely, they gave up after four tries.

Much to his mother's dismay, Carson and his brothers remained single rather than marrying and giving her the daughters-in-law and granddaughters she so desperately wanted.

Carson had toyed with the notion of settling down now that he owned his own ranch. Well, he and the bank owned it.

Uncle Bob had built up the Flying B Ranch from a dozen cows and a hundred acres to more than a thousand acres and a herd any cattleman would envy.

By sheer grit and determination, and the help of faithful ranch hands, Ruth kept the place going since Bob's death in March. When his aunt had called and asked if he'd be interested in purchasing the property, Carson jumped at the opportunity.

His oldest brother would always be first in the chute at the home place. Besides, Carson wanted to make his own mark on the world and he couldn't think of a better place to do it than in Holiday.

Many summers, he'd spent time at the ranch. He even spent three summers while he was in college working for his uncle. During that time, he came to know Bob and Ruth well.

Never blessed with children of their own, his aunt and uncle treated him as if he truly belonged at the ranch. Technically, they were his mother's aunt and uncle, but they'd loved him like a son.

Every minute he spent at the Flying B had been one he treasured. He loved the place even more than the ranch where he grew up and he cared for Ruth like a beloved grandmother.

He'd seen Matilda Dale and her husband, John, many times when he'd been at the Flying B. With all the time he'd spent around them, he wondered why he'd never met Fynlee.

Matilda often spoke of her granddaughter, but Carson always envisioned her as a little girl in pigtails, packing around a stuffed toy or a doll. The notion that she was a beautiful woman close to his age never entered his mind.

Had he met Fynlee Dale, he would have remembered her warm smile and sparkling eyes. Even as a teen, he wouldn't have forgotten her wavy black hair, admirable figure, or alluring voice.

If things were different, Carson might even be interested in asking the lovely girl on a date. She'd certainly monopolized his thoughts the last few days. The echoes of her laughter in his heart and the intriguing hint of her rose-tinged fragrance were to blame for generating his ideas about marriage.

No matter how much Miss Dale interested him, though, he was already involved with someone. His loyalty to that woman was the reason he'd not asked Fynlee out five minutes after he met her.

He'd known Hilary Lytle since kindergarten,

but he hadn't dated her until she returned to their hometown three years ago. After college, she'd worked in Portland for a while but eventually tired of trying to make it on her own. She returned home and sold real estate in her father's office.

Multiple times, she'd tried to get Carson to give up ranching and join them in the business. The last thing he wanted was to be stuck behind a desk or making pushy sales pitches to people.

Sometimes, Carson wondered if he and Hilary had a chance for a future together. Other than going to the same schools and knowing many of the same people, they didn't have much in common. Hilary could be somewhat self-absorbed and focused on wealth and status. Carson didn't like that side of her, although she generally kept it subdued around him.

Despite their differences, he enjoyed dating Hilary and was proud to be with her. Petite, blond, and gorgeous, she looked like a Barbie doll, right down to the designer tan.

Carson scoffed as he mounted Billy, his faithful sidekick and favorite horse. Like a Barbie, he was sure Hilary's generously endowed shape was probably partially plastic or silicone or whatever surgical enhancements women used these days. She didn't look like that in high school. Her hair hadn't been as blond, her teeth as white, or her eyebrows as high. Occasionally, he questioned what about Hilary was real. Of course, he kept those thoughts to himself.

Hilary had begged him not to move to Holiday. She and her father had thrown out a number of tempting offers to keep him from leaving, but Carson had to accept Aunt Ruth's offer.

It was what he'd always wanted and nothing, not even Hilary's flood of tears, would keep him from pursuing his dreams.

He did feel bad about living four hours away from his girl. While it was on his mind, he pulled out his phone and looked up the number of the florist he'd used before. He ordered a bouquet of stargazer lilies and asked the florist to deliver it to Hilary right away.

Impressed with himself that he'd remembered her favorite flower, he hoped the bouquet would help soothe her ruffled feathers. Although she thought he should drop everything and drive home on the weekends, he had far too much work to leave the ranch.

He'd invited her to come to the Flying B, but she'd yet to set foot there.

In the past, Hilary had not shown any interest in the country way of life. If she wanted to have a future with him, though, she'd have to get past her intolerance of ranching and embrace his plans for the Flying B.

Unbidden, a picture of Fynlee riding a horse beside him flashed through Carson's mind. He'd bet his best pair of boots that she wouldn't cringe at a little dust or shake with fright if Billy rubbed his head against her arm.

Fynlee seemed like the type of girl who embraced life's adventures with grace, acceptance, and a good dose of humor.

A wry smile crossed his face as he considered

the colorful force that was Matilda Dale. With her for a grandmother, he'd warrant Fynlee owned long-practiced skills at going with the flow.

Struck with sudden inspiration, Carson decided to run a suggestion by his aunt for her approval. If he assumed correctly, she'd be thrilled with his idea.

Pointedly shifting his focus from the women in his life to the fence line he needed to check, he urged Billy forward into the heat of the afternoon.

Chapter Three

"It's about time you got here," Matilda said, grabbing Fynlee's arm in mid-air.

At the precise moment Fynlee raised her hand to knock on the door, Matilda had opened the portal. After sailing out of her apartment, the old woman hastily slammed the door behind her. A gentle grip returned to Fynlee's arm as she bustled down the hall, pulling the puzzled girl along with her.

Caught off guard, Fynlee followed, wondering what kind of mischief her grandmother had planned now. Rather than head to the elevator, Matilda rushed to Ruth's apartment and tapped on the door. The dozen bracelets on her arm tinkled and clanged, sounding like off-key bells as she rapped again.

The door swung open and Ruth greeted them with a warm smile. "Oh, Fynlee, dear, it's so nice of you to take us."

"Take you? Where are we going?" Fynlee asked. Her gaze traveled between the two older women, hoping one of them would enlighten her.

Ruth offered Matilda a disapproving glance. "Did you forget to tell Fynlee of our plans?"

"I didn't forget, I just hadn't gotten around to it yet," Matilda said, wrapping her arm around Fynlee's waist and giving it a squeeze.

"And what, exactly, are your plans?" Fynlee remained amused yet wary of any schemes her grandmother might have hatched.

"Carson invited us for dinner out at the ranch this evening. Matilda said you'd be happy to drive us. Of course, you're not only invited, but expected to stay for the meal." Ruth picked up a wicker basket and her purse before stepping back out into the hall and closing the door behind her.

Fynlee took the basket from her and followed the two older women to the elevator. Although she'd planned to pop in for a quick visit with Grams then spend the evening catching up on laundry, folding towels could wait another day.

She rarely passed up an opportunity to go out to the ranch. The enticing incentive of seeing Ruth's hunky nephew again dangled before her, leaving her agreeable to the dinner plans.

In the two weeks since she'd met Carson, he'd often dallied in her thoughts. Even though she'd never admit it to anyone, particularly the two old ladies beside her, she'd looked forward to seeing him again.

According to Matilda, he came in to check on Ruth every few days. He'd even arrived Sunday morning to take his aunt to church. Ruth and Carson had attended the small country church near the Flying B. Now that she lived in town, Ruth decided to attend services with Matilda and Fynlee. Carson seemed pleased to join her.

"Do we need to take anything, Grams?" Fynlee asked, wishing her grandmother had given her a little advance notice. If so, Fynlee wouldn't have dawdled after work, visiting with Carrie in the break room. Instead, she would have rushed home and exchanged the slacks and blouse she'd worn to work for a summer dress.

"No, honey. Ruth and I made a salad and a pie today. It's all in the basket." Matilda smiled as Fynlee opened both passenger doors to the backseat of her car. She started it and turned the air conditioner on high then set the picnic basket on the front passenger seat.

From experience, she knew Ruth and Matilda preferred to sit together in the backseat. They liked to pretend Fynlee was their personal chauffeur and she let them.

Once they both were settled inside the car, she shut their doors and slid behind the wheel.

"Music or no today?" she asked, glancing in the rearview mirror at her grandmother.

Matilda looked at Ruth and she nodded her head. "Music please, honey."

While Fynlee preferred soft rock songs, her two passengers loved to listen to big band music. Fynlee kept a few CDs in her car with their favorite tunes and popped in one by Glenn Miller.

Soon the lively sounds of *In the Mood* filled the

car and set the feet of her two passengers to tapping. Fynlee kept time to the beat, drumming her fingers on the steering wheel as she headed out of town toward the Flying B Ranch.

As city streets gave way to wheat fields and pastures full of fat cattle, she felt her shoulders relax and her breathing deepen.

If it wouldn't draw a host of complaints from the backseat occupants, she would have rolled down the window and let fresh air fill the car.

Fynlee drove, pretending not to listen to the two elderly women talk. The conversation between Matilda and Ruth shifted from work Carson had been doing at the ranch to the newest resident of Golden Skies.

"He's taken a shine to you, Ruthie. You can't deny it." Matilda looked at her friend with the same twinkling hazel eyes Fynlee owned.

Ruth demurely brushed a wrinkle out of the skirt of her pale pink cotton dress and shook her head. "Whether he has or not, I'm not interested. Not in the least."

"What's going on, Grams?" Fynlee raised an eyebrow as she glanced back at her grandmother.

"A gentleman moved in last week, a widower. His name is Rand Milton and he is a dandy. He looks like a silver fox."

Fynlee grinned. "A dandy Rand, huh?"

"That he is. From the first evening at dinner, it was perfectly clear he has his eye on Ruth." Matilda ran a hand through her pixie cut hair, still surprisingly dark although it had several streaks of gray. She fluffed it then straightened the mandarin collar of her purple tunic, accented with sequins and embroidered orange flowers along the front.

While Matilda preferred bright colors highlighted with plenty of bling, Ruth chose pastels and understated elegance, like the string of pearls encircling her neck. Her silver hair was fashioned in soft curls that accented her delicate bone structure.

Matilda looked like a vibrant zinnia compared to Ruth's summer rose, but somehow it worked. Fynlee often thought the two women were the most unlikely friends, but they'd been there for each other for nearly fifty years.

Ruth and Bob had been part of her world for as long as she could remember being with Grams and Gramps. She marveled that she'd never run into Carson before he moved to Holiday. Vaguely, she recalled some relative of Bob and Ruth's had worked on the ranch for a few summers. At the time, she'd been in high school and more interested in hanging out with her friends and working at summer camp than spending time with her grandparents' friends.

If that relative had been Carson, she'd really missed out. Back then, he'd probably set every girlish heart he encountered aflutter with the barest hint of that killer smile.

Who was she kidding? Her heart hadn't settled into a regular beat since she'd met him.

"Oh, look, Ruthie!" Matilda pointed out the window at a new sign hanging from the arch across the lane that led to the ranch.

"Carson said he ordered a new sign," Ruth said, craning her neck to see out the window. Fynlee stopped the car and rolled down the window so the two women could get a better view.

She admired the laser-cut metal sign hanging from a thick log twenty-five feet up in the air. Since semi-trucks full of cattle and hay traveled the road, Fynlee knew the sign had to hang high enough to give the top of the loads clearance.

"That's quite a sign," Fynlee commented, rolling up the window and continuing down the drive.

"Carson had me look at the design," Ruth said, sliding back against the seat. "He's so good about asking my opinion, but the ranch is his now. He can do whatever he likes."

"I think he just wants you to be proud of him and to feel involved," Matilda observed, patting Ruth on the knee, and setting her bracelets into a chiming cadence.

"I couldn't be prouder of that boy if he was my own son." Ruth removed a fine linen handkerchief from her handbag and dabbed at her eyes.

Thankfully, before the two women dissolved into tears, Fynlee pulled up in front of the two-story farmhouse. Painted a cheerful shade of yellow with dark green trim, baskets of flowers bloomed from hanging pots and in the planters flanking the porch steps.

Carson jogged down the steps and raised a hand in greeting as she parked the car. Before she could cut the ignition, he'd opened the door to the backseat and tugged his aunt into a hug.

"Hi, Aunt Ruth! It's so good to see you," he said, swinging her around and setting her on the front walk.

She patted his arm and gave him a happy smile. "I love the sign, Carson. It's perfect."

"Glad you think so." He pecked her cheek then hurried around the car.

Fynlee had gotten out and opened the door for her grandmother, but Matilda refused to move. "Come on, Grams."

"Nope. I want the same welcome as Ruth."

Carson laughed and gently pulled her from the car, giving her a hug and escorting her over to where Ruth waited. When he stopped beside his aunt, Matilda squeezed a bulging bicep and waggled her eyebrows at him from behind black round-rimmed glasses that looked like something Harry Potter might wear. "If I was fifty years younger, you'd be in big trouble, young man."

"I'm already in trouble, Miss Matilda." Carson placed a noisy smack to her cheek then turned back to watch as Fynlee took the basket from the front seat and strolled toward them.

A slight prick of jealousy left her disappointed that she didn't get the same treatment from their host as the two older women.

Then again, if Carson had wrapped those impressive arms around her, Fynlee didn't think she'd ever want him to let go. Until she met him, she thought physiques like his were only found on the buff guys who hung out at a gym or in the movies. She had no idea an ordinary man could have such extraordinary muscles.

On second thought, there wasn't anything ordinary about Carson Ford. As he stood with the two old women, Fynlee admired the perfect fit of his jeans.

Heat seared her cheeks and made her freckles stand out at the direction of her thoughts. When Carson took the basket from her hand, she glanced up at him and he winked.

Gallantly, he stepped next to his aunt and held out his arm to her. "Shall we?" he asked.

"We shall," Ruth said, wrapping her hand around his arm and walking inside the refreshing coolness of the house.

"He's so good to her," Matilda whispered to Fynlee as they trailed behind Carson and Ruth through the living room to the kitchen. "Just like you're so good to me."

"Would you rather I treated you like an unwanted pet?" Fynlee offered her grandmother a playful grin.

"No, you smarty." Matilda squeezed her hand as Carson left the basket on the kitchen counter.

He motioned to a table set for four in front of the bay window that looked out over the backyard and the pasture beyond it. A handful of horses grazed there, capturing Fynlee's interest.

"Are those your horses?" she asked, wishing she'd kept her mouth shut. She sounded like a dork. Since Carson owned the ranch, it made sense he'd also own all the animals.

"Yep, they sure are," he said, taking a chocolate cream pie and a bowl of coleslaw out of the basket. He set them on the table then motioned toward the refrigerator. "There's iced tea and lemonade in the fridge if you ladies want to help yourself. Steak and potatoes are on the grill and should be done any minute. There's also a loaf of bread in the oven."

"Good thing I used extra-strength denture glue today," Matilda stage-whispered to Fynlee as Carson carried a platter to the deck outside the kitchen's sliding door.

At her grandmother's words, Fynlee nearly dropped the tea pitcher in her hand. She turned to glare at Matilda, wondering if there was anything the woman wouldn't say or do. Thank goodness, she'd whispered her comment instead of shouting it for all the world to hear.

"Carson's steaks are so tender, you won't have a thing to worry about, Tillie." Ruth patted her friend's arm then opened a cupboard and took down four glasses.

While Fynlee filled them with ice and poured four glasses of iced tea, Ruth and Matilda took the crusty loaf of bread from the oven and set the warm slices in a basket, covering it with a clean dishtowel.

They'd just carried everything to the table when Carson walked inside with the meat and potatoes.

He set the platter on the table and retrieved butter and sour cream from the fridge before taking a seat between the two older women.

At Carson's nod, Ruth offered thanks for the meal. After they all said, "amen," Ruth draped the cloth napkin neatly folded next to her plate over her lap and smiled at her nephew.

"It's nice to see you using the real napkins,

honey."

"Since you left a pile of them here, I assumed that meant you expected me to use them." Carson helped himself to a steak then cut the choicest pieces off two steaks and held the platter out to Matilda. "You and Aunt Ruth take those smaller pieces. They'll be extra tender."

Touched by his considerate behavior toward her grandmother and his aunt, Fynlee observed his attentive care to the older women throughout the meal. When they finished their iced tea, he hopped up to refill their glasses. All the while, he kept up a conversation about work at the ranch and interesting tidbits of news he'd heard around town.

Several times, he looked over at Fynlee, as though checking to make sure she had enough to eat and enjoyed herself. Each time his warm blue gaze met hers, her heart tripped in her chest.

The notions floating through her head, reflections of what it would be like to taste Carson Ford's kiss, left her anxious and nervous. It was pure folly to think such things, but she couldn't seem to stop wondering just the same.

The chocolate pie proved to be a hit with Carson, earning his praise as they each ate a slice. As soon as they finished, Ruth and Matilda volunteered to do the dishes while Carson took Fynlee outside to see the horses.

"I don't want to leave you two to do all the work," Fynlee said, picking up dirty plates and carrying them to the sink.

"It's my house, I should do the dishes," Carson said, setting the pie plate and bowl of coleslaw on the counter.

"No, we insist. You two go on." Matilda gave Fynlee a shove toward the patio door while Ruth made shooing motions at Carson.

He rolled his eyes, but grabbed the straw Stetson he'd left hanging on a peg on the wall then pushed open the patio door. "Ladies first."

Fynlee stepped outside and glanced around, taking in the welcoming appearance of the yard. The fragrance of freshly mown grass and grilled steak lingered in the air, mingling with the musky, earthy aroma of the cowboy beside her. An undertone of rich, dark chocolate made her wonder if it was part of his cologne or a tantalizing hint from the pie they'd just eaten.

It seemed entirely wrong for him to smell so good, especially when it was still ninety-some degrees outside.

While she felt perspiration trickle down her neck and beneath her arm, he appeared cool and confident.

Again, Fynlee wished Grams had given her a little warning about the dinner plans. She would have at least given herself a shot of heavy-duty deodorant and a spritz of her favorite perfume.

"Thank you for including me in the invitation for dinner," she said, following Carson as he walked across the backyard and held open a wooden gate for her. She stepped through and Carson latched it behind her.

They'd only taken a few steps when two dogs raced over to them and yipped at Carson. He hunkered down and patted their heads then scratched their backs.

Fynlee watched, waiting to see if the dogs would welcome her. When one of the red heelers whined and nosed her hand, she decided they were friendly.

"My gosh, Carson, they have such beautiful eyes." She dropped onto her knees and rubbed her hand over the dog's head, admiring eyes the color of a pale winter sky.

"That's Jacques and Octavius, but I call them Jack and Gus."

"Tell me you didn't name your dogs after the mice in *Cinderella*." She couldn't believe Carson would have seen the movie, let alone liked it well enough to name his dogs after two of the fairy tale characters.

"I did not. I got these two from a friend when they were pups. His little girl was obsessed with the movie and named the dogs after the characters. Major, Bruno, and Lucifer were in the litter, too."

Fynlee grinned. "Gus has such incredible eyes."

"Yeah, she does, even if she's stuck with a strange name." Carson rose and gave Fynlee his hand. She took it as she stood, unprepared for the tingling sensation that trailed up her arm and threatened to short-circuit her brain.

He released her fingers and glanced briefly at his hand, causing her to speculate if he felt something, too.

Most likely, it was wishful thinking on her part. It was ludicrous to entertain any ideas about the man, anyway.

Wasn't it?

After all, she barely knew him.

However, from what she'd observed, he was a very kind and patient man, dedicated to his aunt. He'd been equally attentive to her grandmother. Each time she'd encountered him, he'd been easy to talk to and affable.

"So what's your story, Fynlee? Aunt Ruth said you work in an office at the hospital. Is that right?" Carson asked as they neared the pasture fence.

"I work in the billing department. We have our own little building across the parking lot. I'm not sure if it's to keep the germs at bay or to keep the rest of the hospital from hearing the yellers."

"Yellers?" he asked, leaning his arms on the top rail of the fence and glancing at her as she stepped beside him.

"You know, people who don't want to have to pay their bills. They come to the billing office and yell at everyone, hoping that will somehow make the bill magically disappear."

"Sounds like a fun job," Carson said sarcastically.

Fynlee watched as one of the horses broke away from the group and trotted their direction. "It isn't bad. The pay is decent and the hours are good. My boss is nice, but then again, we've been friends since sixth grade. She allows me to start work an hour early so I can leave by four every day to spend time with Grams."

"You seem really close to your grandmother," Carson observed as Billy approached.

The horse moved close to Fynlee, sniffing her

outstretched hand. A sound that could have been a contented sigh floated in the air when she began scratching his neck.

"I am. Grams and Gramps took me in after my parents died when I was just a kid. In some ways, Grams was a grandmother, mother, and friend rolled into one," Fynlee said, admiring the horse. "What's his name?"

"Billy."

"He's a beaut." Fynlee smiled as the horse shifted closer to the fence.

"I thought your grandmother said you went away to college." Carson had no idea why he was digging for information about Fynlee Dale, but he was genuinely interested in her story. He pictured her doing something much more exciting than working in the hospital's billing office. Fashion designer or interior decorator or even something in a field like journalism seemed more her speed.

"I did go to college. In fact, I have a degree in occupational therapy."

Carson looked at her. "What's that?"

"Occupational therapists use a range of activities like art, dance, and theater to assist in the physical or psychological development of children and adults." Fynlee's voice held a note of passion and excitement as she spoke. "I planned to work with children. Therapists can guide a child with cerebral palsy to develop fine motor skills of the hand through drawing or help a little one with autism learn social skills through activities like horseback riding."

"Wow, I had no idea." Carson turned to face

her. "Why aren't you doing that instead of working in the billing office?"

Fynlee released a sigh as she continued giving Billy attention. "I'd just finished my master's degree when Gramps passed away. My plan was to find a job in Portland or Boise, so I'd still be somewhere within driving distance of here. His death hit Grams really hard. She needed me to come home, so I came. In case you haven't noticed, there aren't many job openings here in town, so I took what I could find. It's more important to be with Grams than pursue my career."

Carson couldn't recall the last time he'd met someone as selfless as Fynlee. She'd given up her hopes and dreams to be available for her grandmother. While he admired her loyalty and dedication, he wished she had the opportunity to do something she loved. "Can't you move now? Your grandmother doesn't seem like the type who needs you to stick around and hold her hand."

A laugh bubbled out of her. "No, Grams is definitely not the hand-holding type. If I told her I wanted to leave, she'd help me pack my suitcase and that would be all she wrote." She sobered, taking on a solemn air. "But with Grams getting older, I don't want to be hours away from here and get a call that she…" As she struggled to regain her composure, Fynlee closed her eyes for a moment. "That she… you know, that something happened to her and she was all alone. I need to be here, as much for my own peace of mind as keeping an eye on Grams. It's not easy trying to get her to walk on the straight and narrow path."

Carson eyed her speculatively. "I think keeping your grandmother out of trouble probably takes both eyes and maybe a foot or two, but you're brave to try."

Fynlee laughed again, giving Billy a pat on his neck. The horse decided she didn't have any treats to share with him and wandered back to graze with the other horses. "What about you? What's your story? Why did you move to Holiday?"

"I love it here. Always have. My parents brought us to visit for the first time when I was about seven. From then on, I wanted to be here."

"But doesn't your family have a ranch near Portland?" Fynlee knew a little about Carson from the information she'd heard Grams and Ruth discussing.

"They do, but there are four of us boys and we can't all make a living off the ranch. Eventually, my oldest brother will buy it from my folks, when they're ready to retire. In the meantime, he's second in command under our dad. Sometimes, there are just too many mule-headed Ford men around for things to run as smoothly as they should." Carson leaned against the fence again, watching his horses as the sun started to drop lower in the sky. "I spent several summers here working for Uncle Bob and Aunt Ruth. Those were some of the best months of my life. When Aunt Ruth asked if I'd like to buy the ranch, I couldn't say no. It's been my dream since I was old enough to imagine it being a possibility. When Uncle Bob passed away, I offered to stay with Aunt Ruth, but she said she needed a little time alone to decide what she wanted to do. A month later, she called and asked if I wanted to buy the Flying B."

"Your aunt is so proud of you," Fynlee said, covertly studying Carson as the glow from the sun turned him into a bronzed god from the mythology stories she enjoyed reading as a teen. His blue plaid cotton shirt stretched across the broad expanse of his shoulders and accented the strength of arms.

"I want to make her proud, make her glad she sold me the Flying B. She'll always have a place here, but she was adamant it was time for her to move into town. I think she worried about being a burden to me, but I enjoy having her around. I was hoping if she stayed, Hilary would be more inclined to visit."

"Hilary? Who's that?"

Carson sighed. "My girlfriend. We've been together a few years, but Hilary still hasn't come to terms with my plans to ranch for the rest of my life."

Fynlee couldn't have felt more chilled if someone had dumped a bucket of ice water over her head. All the little fantasies she'd concocted of dating Carson, of someday tasting those luscious-looking lips and being wrapped in his burly arms, crashed around her.

He was spoken for and Fynlee wasn't the type of girl to interfere. Unobtrusively, she put a little distance between them, just far enough his scent didn't completely befuddle her mind.

Clearing her throat along with her thoughts, Fynlee glanced at Carson. "What does Hilary do?"

"She sells real estate in her dad's office, back

in my hometown. We went to school together and I've known her forever. I kind of hoped she'd show a little more interest in the ranch, but so far, she's kept her distance."

"It must be hard on her to have you living four hours away." Fynlee tried to work up some sympathy for the girl he left behind, but failed to find any. If it had been her, Fynlee would have followed Carson anywhere he wanted to go.

"Yeah, I guess." Ready to change the subject, he waved a hand toward the horses. "Anytime you want to ride, just let me know. Aunt Ruth said you used to ride here when you were younger."

"I did. Your uncle was always so kind about saddling one of the gentle horses for me to ride when we'd come out to visit. I haven't ridden since I went away to college. I'm pretty sure I've forgotten everything."

Carson grinned. "I doubt that. It's kind of like riding a bicycle. Once you swing onto the back of a horse, it'll all come back to you." He gave her a warm smile. "I mean it, Fynlee. If you ever want to ride, all you have to do is ask. I'd be happy to help and you've already won over Billy."

"Thanks. I might take you up on that sometime, but I know summer is your busy time of year." Fynlee turned to look at the house. The curtains fluttered as two wrinkled faces hid from view, causing her to smile. "I was surprised you had time to cook dinner for us tonight."

"I needed to eat anyway, and I wanted Aunt Ruth to see the new sign. It was nice of you to drive her out here." Carson stuffed his hands inside his pockets and kept step with Fynlee as they started back to the house.

"I'm more than happy to give her a ride anytime she'd like to come out here. It's good for Grams to get away from Golden Skies, too." Fynlee smiled up at him. "Thank you, again, for including us in the invitation. I think that was the best steak I've ever eaten."

"I'm glad you enjoyed it. Next time, I'll make you the best hamburger you've ever eaten."

"Really? The very best?" Dubious of Carson's claims, she stared at him with obvious skepticism.

"You don't believe me?" he asked.

Fynlee shook her head.

He grinned. "Now I'll have to prove it to you. As soon as wheat harvest is finished, you have to come to dinner."

Despite her head telling her it was a bad idea to spend more time with handsome Carson Ford, Fynlee held out her hand to him. "It's a deal."

Carson shook her hand then opened the patio door and followed her inside.

An hour later, Fynlee walked out to her car after escorting Ruth and Matilda upstairs to their apartments. The two old women stood together in Ruth's living room watching Fynlee hurry across the parking lot to her car.

"We've got to do something about those two," Ruth said, surprising Matilda.

"I was thinking the same thing, but didn't you say Carson's practically engaged to some nitwit?"

"He is. That's exactly why we need to make him fall in love with your girl. She's perfect for him."

"What have you got in mind?" Matilda followed her friend over to the couch and took a seat.

"Well, I was thinking…"

Chapter Four

"I need to go home," Ruth said, clinging to Carson's arm as he escorted her across the church parking lot after the Sunday service.

"What's wrong, Aunt Ruth?" Carson glanced down at her with concern.

"I'm just not feeling well, Carson. I know you planned to have us join you for lunch today, but I really don't feel well."

Carson glanced at Matilda and Fynlee as they headed toward her car, parked a few spaces away from his pickup. He waved a hand at Fynlee to get her attention. When she looked at him, he pointed to Ruth. "I'm going to take Aunt Ruth back to Golden Skies. She isn't feeling well."

"Is there anything we can do to help," Fynlee asked as she and Matilda hurried over to them.

"Gracious, no," Ruth said, smiling at Fynlee. Hastily, her smile faded and she placed a hand to her stomach with a look of discomfort on her face. "I'm sure I just ate something that didn't agree with me. Most likely, it's nothing to worry about."

"I'll take you home, Ruthie," Matilda said, slipping an arm around her friend's waist. "There's no need for you kids to miss out on this beautiful day. Go on and have lunch without us."

"No. That wouldn't be right," Fynlee said, pushing the button on her key fob to unlock her car. Matilda helped Ruth into the front seat then yanked the keys out of Fynlee's hand.

Fynlee reached out to reclaim them, but Matilda held the keys behind her back.

"Grams, I'll take you both to Golden Skies."

Matilda shook her head, making the silver and turquoise chandelier earrings in her ears tinkle like tiny bells. "No, honey. We'll be fine. You go with Carson. He can bring you home after lunch." She turned her focus to the cowboy standing by her granddaughter with a bewildered expression on his face. "You will make sure she gets home okay, won't you, Carson?"

"Yes, ma'am. I mean, I'm happy to take her home, but I think it might be best if…"

Matilda ignored him as she slipped behind the wheel and started Fynlee's car. Carefully backing it out of the space, she drove through the parking lot.

"Grams hasn't driven a car for more than a year. I sure hope she doesn't get in a wreck." Nervous, Fynlee watched as her grandmother pulled onto the street and headed in the direction of the retirement village. It wasn't far, so she hoped Matilda made it with no problem.

"Maybe we should follow them." Carson opened his pickup door and held a hand out to Fynlee.

She accepted it and slid inside, inhaling deeply as the captivating scent of Carson and leather filled her nose.

In the weeks since he'd invited them for dinner, Fynlee had seen him a few times, usually on Sundays. He'd finished the wheat harvest a few days prior and had invited his aunt, Matilda, and Fynlee out to the ranch for lunch after church to celebrate.

Fynlee had both looked forward to going and dreaded it. While she loved being at the ranch and enjoyed Carson's company, it was hard for her to ignore her attraction to the man, especially in his alluring presence. His broad shoulders and big smile made him seem larger than life in the confines of the pickup cab.

Somehow, her grandmother and Ruth had maneuvered to get her alone with Carson. They might convince him otherwise, but she was sure Ruth's sudden illness had nothing to do with anything she ate for breakfast. Most likely, it had everything to do with leaving Fynlee alone with the good-looking cowboy.

As she looked out the passenger window, Fynlee realized Carson had followed Grams all the way to the retirement center. After parking the car, the two women waltzed across the parking lot and inside the building, both appearing to be in high spirits.

"Either Aunt Ruth had a miraculous recovery,

or those two are up to no good." Carson grinned at Fynlee as he continued down the street and turned on the road heading west out of town.

"You really don't have to take me out to the ranch, Carson. It's obvious that Grams and Ruth are plotting something." Fynlee jabbed a thumb over her shoulder in the direction of Golden Skies. "If you let me out here, I can walk back and get my car."

"No can do. There's a reason they didn't want to come out to the ranch today, so we'll leave them be for a few hours. I'll check in on Aunt Ruth when I bring you back to town." Carson sped up as they left Holiday behind them and drove toward the Flying B. "Maybe they're planning something to catch that widower I heard Aunt Ruth mention."

Fynlee grinned. "From what Grams said, your aunt wouldn't have to work very hard to capture him. He's been sweet on Ruth since the day he moved to Golden Skies."

A sudden scowl made lines of concern etch across Carson's forehead. "Have you met him? Does he seem nice?"

"He is a very nice man and oddly enough, he seems well suited to your aunt." Fynlee gave him a knowing look. "When and if she decides she's ready to pay attention to him, he'll be waiting."

His voice sounded protective when he spoke. "It may be awhile before Aunt Ruth is interested. Uncle Bob's passing hit her really hard."

Fynlee nodded. "I know it did. I think Grams mostly just likes to tease her about Mr. Milton's infatuation with her. You know how she is."

Carson's good humor returned and he chuckled. "Your grandma is good for my aunt. She helps her not take life so seriously."

"I'd like to say your aunt is good for Grams, helping her to be more dignified and ladylike, but…"

They both laughed.

"Miss Matilda is one of a kind, that's for sure." He turned off the highway onto the lane leading to the ranch.

"That's a nice way to put it, Carson. Most people think Grams is a marble or two short of a full bag, but she has a big heart and a fun way of viewing life."

"I think that's important. It's nice you accept her the way she is." He parked the truck near the front walk and shut off the ignition. "I guess I should have asked if you preferred to eat out, but I've already got the stuff ready for those hamburgers I promised you."

"No, this is great," Fynlee said, impulsively reaching out and squeezing his hand. A jolt, like she'd been zapped with an electrical charge, made her entire arm tingle before she released his fingers. "Thank you for bringing me out here."

"Like I said, you're welcome anytime. Now that wheat harvest is over and things aren't quite as busy, drive out some evening and ride with me." Carson ran around the pickup and opened the passenger door, offering her his hand.

Fynlee took it, ready for the second jolt that hit her as she slid off the seat. Immediately, he released her hand and motioned for her to precede him up the porch steps. He opened the door to the house. The coolness felt welcoming in contrast to the heat of the day.

"Make yourself at home," Carson said, closing the door behind her and pointing toward the kitchen. "I'm gonna run upstairs and change, but feel free to pour yourself a glass of tea."

"Thanks." Fynlee watched him take the stairs two at a time. By force of will, she shut down thoughts of how good he looked in those pressed dark blue jeans with a dress shirt the same shade of blue as his eyes and a dark gray tie. Instead, she let her gaze travel around the living room. It looked much as it had when Ruth lived there. A leather couch and a big recliner took the place of the floral upholstered couch and side chair Ruth had taken with her to the apartment at Golden Skies.

Fynlee wandered into the kitchen and removed two glasses from the cupboard. She filled both with ice then reached into the fridge to get the pitcher of tea. As she turned to pour the liquid, she noticed a photograph in a sleek black frame sitting on the counter.

Quickly filling the glasses, she set down the tea pitcher and lifted the frame, studying the beautiful woman in the photo. From the top of her blonde head to the perky hint of her bustline, the woman in the photo looked like a perfect replica of a classic Barbie doll — little button nose, amazingly straight teeth, huge blue eyes, and every platinum hair in place.

With a sigh, Fynlee carefully placed the photograph back on the counter and took a long drink of her tea. It was no wonder Carson had fallen for Hilary. She wasn't just pretty, but model-on-the-runway gorgeous.

The hurried sound of his footsteps trailed into the kitchen as he clattered down the back stairs and appeared with a smile.

"Let's get those burgers cooking," Carson said, taking pre-formed patties out of the refrigerator and setting them on the counter. He hurried outside and fired up the grill then returned inside.

He set a few potatoes by the sink along with a sharp knife. "Can you slice those into wedges?"

"Sure. What are we making?" Fynlee asked as he turned on the oven and lined a baking sheet with foil.

"My special fries." Carson poured a little olive oil in a resealable bag then added a dash of salt, pepper, and seasoning. When she finished slicing the potatoes, he placed them in the bag and gave it a good shake to coat every surface.

"And the special fries are to go along with the best burgers I'm ever going to taste. Right?" She watched as he spread the potatoes on the foil-lined baking sheet and slid it into the oven.

"Exactly." The grin that crinkled his eyes at the corners tugged at her heart. Boyish and charming, he was also rugged and undeniably masculine. How could anyone resist such an enthralling combination? It seemed entirely unfair that she had to do exactly that.

Carson took the burgers outside and placed them on the grill.

Fynlee stood at the door, studying the way his

faded blue T-shirt stretched across his shoulders and his worn Wranglers were snug in all the right places. The foolish inappropriateness of her thoughts left her convicted and she dropped her gaze.

"What can I do to help?" she asked as he returned inside and washed his hands.

"You can set the table while I get out the rest of the stuff." He opened the refrigerator again, setting ketchup, mayonnaise, lettuce, and pickles on the counter. "I'd offer you onions, but I can't stand the taste or smell of them."

Fynlee looked over her shoulder at him as she set two plates on the table. "I'm not fond of them either. Grams used to add them liberally to everything. I shouldn't admit it, but I was relieved when they started giving her indigestion and she had to stop cooking with them."

Chuckles filled the room as Carson sliced a ripe tomato then set it aside. "I won't tell if you don't let Aunt Ruth know how glad I was she took her flowered furniture with her when she moved. It's a little too girly for my taste."

"My lips are sealed." Fynlee winked at him as she set the condiments on the table.

When she turned around, Carson stared at her, the knife poised in mid-air above a block of cheese.

Self-consciously, she looked down to make sure she hadn't spilled something on her dress or some similar disaster.

She glanced back at Carson, but his attention was focused on slicing cheese. "I think I'll go freshen up a bit," she said, wandering down the hall to the guest bathroom.

Purposely keeping his eyes glued to the cheese in front of him, Carson released a long sigh when Fynlee disappeared down the hall.

"Get it together man," he muttered to himself, as he hurried outside to flip the burgers. Each time he saw Fynlee, he felt drawn to her in ways that defied any reasonable explanation. Part of him had wanted to cheer when his aunt and Matilda bailed on lunch plans at the last minute, giving him the afternoon alone with Fynlee.

The photo of Hilary caught his eye when he returned inside the kitchen. Without a moment of hesitation, he picked up the frame and tossed it into the junk drawer. The professional portrait of her had arrived in yesterday's mail. He'd set it on the counter and not given it another glance.

As any number of thoughts about Fynlee trickled through his mind, the last thing he wanted was a photo of his supposed girlfriend sitting around, prodding at his guilt.

In all fairness, he hadn't made any promises or commitments to Hilary. She was free to date whomever she liked. He'd certainly given ample consideration to dating Fynlee.

Before he took that step, though, he wanted to reach a firm decision about his relationship with Hilary. He wasn't the type of man to string two women along while he made up his mind about which one he liked best.

Admittedly, the scale continued tipping in Fynlee's favor. Not only had Hilary been exceedingly irritating lately with a never-ending string of needy text messages, every time the opportunity arose, she whined about him moving back home.

In truth, Carson hadn't missed her as much as he probably should have, but he'd been so busy with the ranch, he hadn't had much time to think about Hilary.

Especially not when visions of Fynlee constantly filled his head.

Frustrated with himself, Carson scrubbed a hand over his face then took two buns out of the package on the counter. It had been all he could do to keep his eyes off Fynlee the moment she and Matilda walked into church that morning. With her dark hair gathered into a bun at the back of her head and a white cotton dress accenting her exquisite figure, she looked like an ideal picture of both womanhood and summer.

The wink she'd tossed his way a few minutes ago nearly caused him to slice through his finger. Entranced by the fun sparkle in those hazel eyes and the freckles dancing across her nose, he hadn't paid attention to what he was doing. For a crazy second, he considered what it would be like to savor her delectable lips.

Carson knew he needed to get past this attraction to Fynlee or break up with Hilary. It wasn't fair to anyone for him to waver between his feelings for both women.

However, for the duration of one simple lunch together, it couldn't hurt to indulge in the fantasy that he and Fynlee were unattached and interested in each other.

No matter what else happened, Carson counted Fynlee among his friends. He valued her opinion, enjoyed their conversations, and eagerly anticipated the sound of her laughter. No matter the state of his heart, he didn't want to do anything to mess up their friendship.

Before he had time for further speculation, she returned to the kitchen. Her fragrance tickled his nose, bringing to mind the fluffy flowers Aunt Ruth liked.

Peonies. That was the name.

Fynlee's fragrance smelled like peonies with a hint of something that put him in mind of cashmere.

Peonies and cashmere?

He was really losing it.

Intent on clearing his mind, he focused on lunch preparations.

"The burgers will be ready in a minute. Would you mind checking the fries?" he asked. "When they're done, dump them into that bowl and give everything a good stir, then pop the spuds back in the oven for a few minutes." He carried a plate outside with cheese slices, buns, and strips of bacon he'd cooked that morning.

Fynlee found a potholder and checked on the fries. They looked crispy and cooked to perfection, so she removed them from the oven and carefully slid them into a large bowl Carson left on the counter near the stove. Parmesan cheese and chopped parsley coated the bottom. Picking up a spoon next to the bowl, she stirred until the potatoes were coated then spooned them back onto the baking sheet. She returned it to the oven and waited.

Carson stepped inside with two burgers and slid one onto her plate then set the other on his.

"Are your taste buds ready to tap dance?" he asked with a grin. Quickly, he rinsed his hands then he held out a chair for her.

Dazed by his mannerly gesture, Fynlee took her seat and nodded her head. The few guys she'd dated never held doors, chairs, or exhibited any gentlemanly traits. For the most part, they acted like a bunch of cavedwellers.

After Carson said grace, Fynlee broke off a little piece of the hamburger and popped it in her mouth.

"You weren't kidding. That is the best burger I've ever tasted," she said, grinning at Carson as she added mayo, lettuce, pickles, and tomato slices to her burger.

"I don't kid about beef," Carson said, retrieving the fries from the oven. He gave Fynlee a scoop of fries before placing a serving on his plate.

Fragrant steam wafted up from a fry as she bit into it. Her eyes widened in surprise. "These fries are amazing. What did you use to season them?"

Carson wiped his mouth on a napkin before answering. "I season the potatoes with salt, pepper, and a little powdered ranch dressing mix. Before I bake them, I give them a coating with olive oil. When they're done, I toss them with parsley and Parmesan cheese. That's it."

"But they are so, so good," Fynlee said, eating another fry. It was a good thing she didn't eat Carson's cooking with any frequency or she'd gain fifty pounds. "How'd you learn to cook?"

He grinned at her. "My mother was determined to teach someone domestic arts, as she calls it. With no girls in our family, she made all of us boys learn to cook, clean, and do laundry. As much as we hated it at the time, it's been handy to have those skills as an adult."

"I like the way your mother thinks." Fynlee took another bite of her burger. As they ate, they chatted about how Ruth had adjusted to life at the retirement village and how much Matilda enjoyed her presence there. Fynlee shared funny stories from things that had happened to her at work and Carson talked about a few near disasters that occurred during harvest.

Once they finished the meal and Fynlee helped Carson with the dishes, they wandered outside.

"You're apt to get those pretty shoes all dirty out here," Carson said, glancing down at the white eyelet sandals Fynlee wore.

"It's okay." She was much more interested in petting the dogs and seeing the horses than worrying about grass stains on her shoes.

"Wait here a minute."

Carson disappeared inside the house and soon returned with a worn pair of cowboy boots and a pair of thick socks. "Try these on. They belonged to Uncle Bob, but he had a small foot for a guy."

Fynlee sat down on a padded deck chair and removed her sandals then pulled on the socks and boots. Although they were a little big, the boots would suffice as long as she didn't have to participate in any foot races.

"These will work. Thanks." She set her sandals

inside the house then rejoined Carson as he wandered toward the horse pasture.

Gus and Jack ran out from the barn, barking excitedly.

"You two stay down," Carson warned when the dogs started to jump up on Fynlee.

She leaned over and gave them both loving attention, making Carson marginally jealous. As she rubbed a hand over Jack's head, he wondered what it would feel like to have her long fingers run through his hair.

Abruptly derailing those thoughts before they gathered any steam, he grabbed Fynlee's hand in his. "Come on. I've got an idea."

A short while later, Fynlee stared from Carson to the horse in front of her. "I don't know about this. I think we should wait until I'm at least wearing pants."

"I'd let you borrow a pair of mine, but I know they wouldn't fit that fine figure of yours. You'd swim in them. The dress you're wearing should work well enough," Carson assured her, tightening the cinch on Billy.

He'd caught the gentlest horse he owned, one Uncle Bob had trained from a colt. Peanut was as sweet as they came and would be a great mount for Fynlee as she reacquainted herself with the joys of riding.

The comment about her figure left her ill at ease and oddly gratified at the same time. Coupled with her growing anxiety about riding, her stomach clenched from nerves. "Really, Carson, I'm not dressed for this and…"

"There's no one out here but you and me and besides, your skirt's long." He glanced down at the flowing fabric that covered her long legs, ending mid-calf. "I promise if you are indecently exposed, I'll let you know."

Fynlee rolled her eyes and released an exasperated sigh. "That sounds like something Grams would say. You wouldn't believe how many times similar statements have led to profound embarrassment for me."

Carson smirked. "I can imagine." He led Peanut over to a bale of straw and motioned for Fynlee to stand on it.

She took the hand he held out to her and stepped up, then placed a foot in the stirrup. "Close your eyes until I get settled," she said, casting an anxious glance his direction before swinging her right leg over the saddle.

Carson closed his eyes for a few seconds then opened them as Fynlee tucked the hem of her skirt beneath her thighs in the front. Somehow, she'd managed to wrap the material around her legs so it looked like she wore some sort of old-fashioned bloomers. He'd at least hoped to glimpse a little flash of skin above her knee, but no such luck.

He handed her Peanut's reins then swung onto Billy. "Are you ready?"

"Lead the way, cowboy."

They rode for more than an hour before Carson noticed Fynlee wince when the horse took a bouncing step across a ditch.

"Let's head back to the house," he said, realizing they'd been out far longer than he'd planned. Fynlee was so fun to be around and she'd enjoyed the ride so much, he'd not given a thought to her becoming sore, especially wearing a dress instead of jeans.

Normally, he would have been careful to keep a new rider from overdoing it. However, the excitement and pleasure she'd shown in the opportunity to ride jumbled his common sense.

The sight of her dark hair tumbling out of the bun on her head and cascading in shiny waves down her back had created an undeniable desire to run his fingers through the tresses. Visions of taking her in his arms and kissing her senseless scrambled his ability to possess a rational thought.

As soon as they arrived at the barn, Carson swung out of the saddle and hurried around Billy over to Fynlee.

She started to swing a leg over the saddle, but her skin seemed stuck to the leather.

"Do you need help?" he asked, uncertain what he could do.

"This will hurt like ripping off a Band-Aid, but fast is probably going to be less painful." She tried to stand in the stirrups, but still seemed glued to the seat of the saddle.

Carson placed his hands on her waist, ready to assist. "On the count of three. One. Two…" He lifted and swung her out of the saddle, cringing at the yelp that escaped her. He set her on the ground but kept his hands at her waist.

"What happened to three?" Accusation mingled with amusement and a hint of pain in her expressive face as she shook out her skirt. It was stuck to her in places it shouldn't be and wrinkled beyond redemption.

"I thought you'd tense up on three and it would be easier this way. Want me to take a look?" Carson bent down and reached for the hem of her dress.

Fynlee took a step away from him, barely suppressing a groan. "No. I don't think that's a good idea. It's past time for me to get back to town, anyway."

"Are you sure I can't help you, Fynlee? I'd be happy to look things over." At his playful smirk, Fynlee knew he was teasing.

"I assure you that your assistance is completely unnecessary. Besides, you need to take care of the horses. While you do that, I'll change my shoes and get ready to go."

"Okay, Rosie Posie."

Fynlee had started toward the house but stopped and turned back to Carson, glowering at him. "What did you call me?"

"Rosie Posie. Your grandmother mentioned your middle name is Rose. She said you loved that nickname when you were in school."

"Oh, did she? I'll have to make sure to thank her for that." Fynlee continued scowling. "I don't suppose she mentioned the kids all tormented me with that name when I was eleven and had a sudden growth spurt that left me towering above everyone, including the boys. They used to gather around me and sing that horrible *Ring Around the Rosie* song."

Carson appeared appropriately shamed. "I'm sorry. I didn't know."

Fynlee gave him a curt nod then turned back

toward the house.

"For what it's worth, you still seem rather rose-like to me." Carson grinned when she glared at him over her shoulder.

"Rose-like indeed," Fynlee muttered as she made her way into the house. More like a prickly thorn or a wild blossom.

Between the unfamiliar stretching of muscles she hadn't used in a long time, the bunched fabric of her skirt, and the spots where her skin had sweat and stuck to the leather of the saddle, she was in real pain.

At the door, she traded the boots for her sandals then limped into the bathroom. Gingerly lifting her skirt, the sight of three oozing sores caused her to grimace.

"Not good. Not good at all." Rather than ravage Carson's medicine cabinet for ointment and bandages, she decided to attend to the sores at home. As fast as she could force herself to walk, she returned to the kitchen.

Carson stepped inside and washed his hands. "I started the truck so it will cool down. Do you think we should take anything to Aunt Ruth and your grandma?"

"I'm sure they're fine. Grams will have gotten Ruth whatever she needed, if, in fact, she was sick."

"Yeah, I'm still not convinced there was anything wrong with her. I guess we'll soon find out."

Fynlee was quiet on the way back to town. She kept shifting on the seat and Carson couldn't help but notice she held her skirt out so the air from the floor vents blew beneath the hem.

"Are you okay?" he asked, concerned as much by her quietness as her behavior.

"I'm fine."

When she kept her eyes glued on the passing landscape, Carson was sure she wasn't fine. He should have known better than to convince her to ride in the dress, but he'd wanted to spend more time with her and give her the opportunity to do something she'd enjoyed as a girl.

"Did you not enjoy riding?" he finally asked.

Her head whipped around and she held his gaze. "It was awesome, Carson. Peanut is a sweetheart, and it was so nice of you to take me for a ride."

"I'm relieved to hear that. I thought maybe you had a horrible time and won't ever come out to the ranch again."

"No. I had a fabulous time. Those really were the best fries and burgers I've ever had." Pain flashed across her face when Carson hit a pothole in the road.

He grabbed for her skirt and started to lift the hem. She smacked at his hand. "What do you think you're doing?"

"Finding the cause of what's hurting you. Did you get a saddle sore?" His fingers tugged at her skirt.

At another tap on his wrist, he let go of her dress, but his hand settled on her arm with a gentle touch, leaving her more discombobulated than when he'd tried to lift her skirt.

She stared out the window. "I did not get a

saddle sore."

He studied her a moment. "How many?"

Silence met his question.

"Fynlee?" He took her chin in his hand, forcing her to meet his gaze. "How many?"

"Three." A flush stole up her neck and seared her face, making the freckles stand out on her nose and cheeks.

"I'm so sorry, Fynlee. This is my fault."

"No, it's not," she said, taking his hand between hers and squeezing it. Forcefully ignoring the lightning bolts created by the contact, she fused her gaze to his. "This afternoon was one of the nicest, most wonderful days I've had in a long time. That's because of you, Carson."

"You're welcome, but I am sorry about those sores."

He turned into the parking lot of a ranch supply store and parked. "Wait here. I'll just be a minute."

Only a few moments passed when he returned and handed Fynlee a small brown bag. "Go home and take a shower then rub that on the sores. It'll help them heal faster."

She peeked in the bag and removed a tin of salve used to treat cows' udders. The look she shot at Carson made him laugh.

"Hey, don't knock it until you try it. That salve is great for all kinds of problems. Just try it tonight and if it doesn't help, I'll tell you the nickname I had in school that I hated."

"That's a deal," she said, wondering what nickname Carson could have possibly had. She imagined something along the lines of hunkalicious or beefcake.

Carson pulled into the Golden Skies parking lot and found a space close to Fynlee's car. "I can tell your grandmother you needed to get home if you don't want to go in."

Fynlee shook her head and stuffed the tin of salve into her purse. "Grams has my car keys and even if she didn't, she'll call me fourteen times this evening if I don't at least pop in for a minute."

"Let me help you out." Carson jogged around his truck and lifted Fynlee off the seat, setting her down next to him before offering her his arm. "I'd be happy to carry you inside."

The fact that he could so effortlessly lift her had amazed her every time it happened. Fynlee would have relished the opportunity to linger in his arms, but that would only make it harder to stay away from him.

Even though she'd pretended all afternoon that Carson was unattached, the truth remained that he had a girl who loved him.

"I appreciate the offer, but I can walk," she said, taking his arm. Slowly, they made their way inside Golden Skies and up to the third floor.

They'd barely stepped off the elevator when Matilda poked her head outside of her apartment door and smiled at them. "Oh, hello! Did you two have fun?"

"We sure did, Miss Matilda. How about you and Aunt Ruth?" Carson hid his smile as his aunt opened her door and started down the hall looking perfectly healthy until she caught sight of him. Hastily backtracking, she quietly closed her door.

By the time he got to her apartment, she'd no doubt be reclining on the couch with a cool compress on her head.

"She's doing as well as can be expected. Perhaps she had a touch of the flu," Matilda suggested as Fynlee gave Carson a knowing look.

"I'm sure she had a touch of something," he agreed. "You ladies enjoy the rest of your day." With a tip of his hat, he walked to Ruth's door and tapped once before opening it and disappearing inside.

Fynlee followed her grandmother inside her apartment and retrieved her car keys. Although Matilda wanted her to sit down and chat, all Fynlee wanted was to find relief from the burning sores making her thighs feel like they were about to catch fire.

"I promise I'll give you all the details another day, Grams, but I really must go home. Do you need anything before I leave?"

Matilda affectionately patted her cheek. "No, honey. I'm glad you had a good time. I'll see you tomorrow."

"Yes, you will, Grams. You and Ruth stay out of trouble."

At Fynlee's warning glance, Matilda shrugged with feigned innocence. "Of course, dear."

As Fynlee drove home, she figured it wouldn't be long before Grams steered Ruth into more mischief.

Chapter Five

Carson stared at Fynlee, convinced he'd misheard her. "They're planning what?"

"A harvest party in your barn. They didn't mention it to you? Ruth said she and Bob used to host them all the time when they first wed." Fynlee reined Peanut to a stop.

After she recovered from her initial horseback experience with Carson, she'd been out to the ranch several times to ride with him. Each time she rode, she grew more confident in her abilities to handle the horse while falling harder for the handsome cowboy who owned the Flying B.

"A harvest party? In my barn?" Carson removed his Stetson and ran a hand through his hair. Despite keeping it short, it was thick, tousled, and nearly irresistible to Fynlee. Her hand itched so badly to run through it, she rubbed her palm against the denim of her jeans to relieve the twinge.

"Grams said she and Ruth planned it for the Saturday before Halloween. I think they've even sent out invitations."

Carson grunted and muttered something Fynlee couldn't hear. Finally, he turned to her with a perturbed look. "What is it with your grandmother and my aunt? It's like they can't stay out of trouble."

"Don't ask me. Grams gets into enough messes on her own, but together it's like turning two toddlers loose in a candy factory."

Carson chuckled as they continued on the path around the pond toward the barn. "I bet the residents and staff at the Hokey Pokey Hotel have no idea what hit them since those two combined forces."

Fynlee giggled so hard she almost fell out of the saddle. "Hokey Pokey Hotel? Is that what you call Golden Skies?"

"Only when I'm out of earshot of Aunt Ruth." Carson smirked. "It seems like a fitting title."

"That it does." Fynlee tried to curtail her laughter, but when Carson waggled his eyebrow at her, a fresh round assailed her.

She was still laughing when they rode up to the barn. One of Carson's hired hands gave her a strange look as he took the horses from them.

"You better wind that down, Rosie Red, before one of the nosy old women in the house catch sight of you."

Despite Fynlee's protests at the name, Carson had dubbed her Rosie Red and called her that at every opportunity. He claimed he liked her middle name, red was her best color, and she put him in mind of roses.

Had it been anyone else uttering the moniker, she would have hated it. However, the sound of his deep, rumbling voice saying the name never failed to make a delightful shiver work its way from her head to her toes.

She had yet to discover the nickname he hated, but she figured given enough time she'd unearth the truth.

"You've got bigger problems to worry about, buster. Like hosting a harvest party you didn't even know you were having." Fynlee snatched the cowboy hat from Carson and settled it on her dark head. She walked backward toward the door, giving him a teasing grin. "If you don't start paying attention, there'll be no end to the havoc Ruth and Grams will wreak around here."

Briefly stopping to give Gus and Jack some attention, she raced up the porch steps and inside the house.

Carson watched her go, admiring the way her jeans fit just right, how her legs seemed a mile long in her cowboy boots, and how much he cared for her.

If he weren't already in a relationship with Hilary, it would be so easy to fall for Fynlee Rose Dale.

"I can't believe they talked me into doing this,"

Carson said as he looked around his barn.

"Don't worry. It'll be fun," Fynlee said, squeezing his hand.

Fynlee had driven out every evening that week to help him get ready for the party. Although he tried to cancel it, his aunt assured him that was impossible since she and Matilda had already sent out invitations and hired a band.

Carson had his hired hands clean the barn from top to bottom and remove anything that might either get in the way or be carried off without them knowing. They built a platform across one end of the barn for the band to play on and set up sawhorses with plywood for the food and beverage tables.

Fynlee took him out to a pumpkin patch and they loaded his truck. Between straw bales, the pumpkins, and cornstalks she'd tied into artful bunches with orange baling twine, things looked festive at the old barn.

She'd arrived early that morning with boxes of white Christmas lights she'd somehow talked Golden Skies into letting her borrow. Strings of lights crisscrossed the barn rafters and surrounded the doors, casting a warm glow over the entire area.

When they finished, Fynlee made gallons of punch while Carson grilled beef roasts they planned to slice and serve with warm rolls for simple sandwiches.

Aunt Ruth and Matilda had volunteered to oversee the desserts and offered to be greeters at the door.

Fynlee ran into town to pick up the two women

and their desserts while Carson grabbed a shower.

Ruth greeted her wearing a Mrs. Claus costume that fit her personality perfectly. Fynlee needed a moment to compose herself when Matilda appeared dressed in a Carmen Miranda costume, complete with the hat of fruit on her head.

"Grams, are you sure you'll be warm enough in that?" Fynlee wondered what sort of crazy person had looked at her grandmother and decided it would be a good idea to sell her the costume.

At least it wasn't one with a bare midriff. If it had been, Fynlee would have refused to let Matilda go to the party. As it was, the woman had on bright pink leggings, visible along the thigh-high split in the dress and a lime green turtleneck beneath the many ruffles of the strapless top.

Colorful. Grams was definitely colorful.

As the two women settled themselves in her car, Fynlee made multiple trips to carry down the sweets they'd baked.

She rushed back out to the Flying B Ranch and bit her cheek to hold back a laugh when Carson gaped at her grandmother as she sashayed down the front walk and up the porch steps.

He caught Fynlee's eye and winked at her as he hugged the two old women and escorted them inside.

Fynlee drove her car around to the barn so they could set the desserts out on the tables she'd draped with black coverings.

"You should have sent me a text to warn me about your grandmother," Carson said as he helped her unload four cakes, six pies, and dozens of cookies.

"That would have entirely ruined the shock value." She smiled at him over her shoulder. "As soon as we finish here, you better put on your costume. You'll have to keep an eye on Grams and Ruth while I run home to change."

"I thought you were going to get ready here." Carson set the last pie on the table and shut the door to the barn to keep the dogs out. The last thing they needed was Gus or Jack jumping on one of the tables. The barn cat and her babies had already been moved to the hay shed until after the party.

"I was, but I decided it would probably take less time for me to run home and get ready than to pack up everything I need and do it here," Fynlee said, motioning for Carson to get in her car. She drove back to the house and followed him inside. "Hurry up and change and I'll help you with your makeup."

"Makeup?" he asked, backing toward the stairs. "No one said anything about makeup."

Hazel eyes rolled back and she offered him an exasperated sigh. "Just go put on your costume."

Fynlee waited five minutes before calling up the stairs. "Carson? Are you dressed?"

When he failed to answer, Ruth appeared and gave her a nudge forward. "Go on up, dear. I'm sure he's had plenty of time to change."

Although she'd only been upstairs a few times, she knew Carson's room was the last door down the hall — the master suite.

When she tapped on the door, he pulled it open and scowled at her. "I look like an idiot."

Fynlee's eyes widened while her mouth flooded with moisture at the sight of his bulging muscles and suntanned skin. The urge to reach out and touch his bicep was so strong, that she clasped her hands together behind her back.

Without time to track down a great costume, she'd suggested he choose something easy like a mechanic or a cowboy.

Since Carson was a cowboy and dressed that way every day, he decided to go with a construction worker. He'd found an old hard hat in the shop. With a pair of lace-up work boots, faded jeans, a white muscle shirt, and a tool belt fastened around his hips, it was a simple costume to assemble.

"An idiot is not the first word that comes to mind," she said, walking in a circle around him, ogling him from every angle.

"What comes to mind then? Colossal moron?" Carson fidgeted under her intense perusal, uncertain what the look on her face or the fiery light in her eyes meant.

There was no way in the world Fynlee would voice the thoughts that came to her mind. They started with hunky hottie and ran the full gamut right down to sexy cowboy in a totally tempting construction worker costume.

"How about good-natured nephew who loves his aunt and her wacky friend so much, he'd subject himself to this Halloween party?"

"Harvest festival. Aunt Ruth wants to call it a harvest festival, even though we all have to wear costumes and there's a bushel basket full of candy out in the barn for the kids." Carson glanced at

Fynlee as she stepped in front of him with a makeup bag in hand. "What are you planning to do with that?"

"Nothing. I was going to give you a zombie or vampire look, but with that rakish stubble, I think you'll do quite nicely just as you are."

Carson rubbed a hand over his whiskers. "I'm not sure I've shaved at all since church last Sunday. This week has been something of a blur."

She started to tell him he'd shaved Wednesday when he took Ruth to her doctor's appointment, but refrained. That might tip him off to the fact she paid attention to such matters.

Resigned to being just friends, Fynlee couldn't help it if her heart desperately wanted more. So much more.

The intense longing she felt to know Carson's love threatened to ruin her evening, so she tamped it down and pasted on a smile. "I can turn you into a ghost if you like."

Carson shook his head. "I'll pass, but thanks for the offer." He gave her a long glance. "Unless you're planning to show up at this shindig as a harried party planner, you better put some hustle in it and change."

"I'm on my way." Fynlee hurried downstairs and out to her car. She raced back to town, took a shower in record time and styled her hair. Quickly applying makeup, she dressed in her costume and headed out the door. A text from Carson asked her to pick up more ice on her way to the ranch, so she made a quick detour to the grocery store and grabbed four bags.

Cars were pulling up the driveway as she returned to the Flying B. Pleased to see it would be a good turnout, she parked by the house, leaving the parking spaces closer to the barn for those who shouldn't walk as far.

Matilda and Ruth had invited all the residents of Golden Skies as well as many of their former neighbors and friends. They'd also included everyone from church, Fynlee's friends, and the friends Carson had made since taking over the ranch.

As guests arrived, Fynlee shoved a tube of lipstick, a package of gum, and her cell phone in one pocket, her car keys in another, then slid her purse beneath the front seat. She grabbed the ice, locked the car, and rushed toward the barn.

Matilda and Ruth both stood from their seats by the door and hugged her, admiring her costume. In an effort to surprise the two old dears, she refused to tell them or Carson what she planned to wear.

"Oh, that's perfect for you, sweetheart. Just perfect," Ruth gushed. "Wait until Carson sees you."

"Where is our mister tall, hunky and handsome?" Grams asked, glancing around the barn.

"He was over at the food table slicing beef. Carson asked if you could help him when you returned, Fynlee." Ruth pointed toward the long food table at the back of the barn.

"Sure, Ruth. I'd be happy to do that." Fynlee smiled and greeted people as she made her way through the barn, carrying two bags of ice in each hand.

When she approached the table, she grinned at Carson and held up the bags of ice. "Where do you want these?"

The quick glance he cast at her turned into a long second look. Awestruck, he continued staring at her. Absently, he wondered if he'd started to drool.

"Ice, Carson. Where should I put the ice?" Fynlee moved around the table to stand beside him.

Numbly, he flipped the lid open on a large cooler and took the bags from her. When he closed the lid and turned around, she placed her frigid hands on his bare arms. If he hadn't been so overheated from seeing her, he might have said something to tease her.

As it was, her cool hands on his feverish skin just made him want to wrap his arms around her and kiss all that velvety red lipstick off her pretty mouth.

Finally finding his voice, he grinned. "Wow, Fynlee. That costume is so perfect for you," he said, studying her from the red and white polka-dot bandana tied around her black curls to the black lace-up boots on her feet. "Rosie the Riveter for my gorgeous Rosie Red."

The dark blue work shirt and cargo pants she wore fit her like a glove, and he couldn't help but admire the view. She'd even turned the hem of the pants up to show off the bright red socks she wore. The way she'd rolled her shirtsleeves accented the toned length of her arms.

Of its own accord, his hand reached out and

rubbed up and down the soft skin of her arm then captured her fingers with his. "You look amazing."

Fynlee grinned and dipped into a curtsey. "Thank you, kind sir." As she stood, her eyes locked with his and she took a stumbling step forward, right into his solid chest.

"You okay?" he whispered, brushing a springy curl out of her eye.

"Yeah." Although her head nodded up and down, she was far from okay. The look in Carson's eyes, the enticing scent of him, and the exquisite feeling of being held against the wall of muscle that was his chest made her so lightheaded, she thought she might swoon.

Swoon?

Obviously, she'd been listening to too many of Matilda and Ruth's stories.

Everything in her wanted to stay right there in Carson's arms the rest of the night. However, the steady stream of people entering the barn would soon be ready to eat, and they had food to serve.

Determined to keep a tight grip on her feelings for Carson, she stepped away from him and pointed to the beef he'd been slicing. "What can I do to help?"

Twenty minutes later, all the food was ready. The barn was packed with guests. Youngsters played the games Fynlee had set up in some of the empty stalls, supervised by a few of the teens from church.

Carson located their pastor, who had arrived dressed as a hobo, and asked him to offer the blessing for the meal.

As soon as the last "amen" was uttered, Carson took the microphone and welcomed everyone to the party. He invited the guests to fill their plates and enjoy their evening.

Ruth and Matilda led the food line, taking their plates back to their table by the door.

Fynlee hovered near the food table, filling empty platters and visiting with guests. Carson spoke with the band, helped Sage from Golden Skies find seats for all the residents she'd brought in the activity bus, and carved more meat when the platters he filled ran out.

Several times, he glanced over at Fynlee, watching the way she made people feel welcome and important. A light shined inside her that spilled onto others, wrapping them in her special glow.

No more immune to it than anyone else, Carson wanted to be closer to that light, to bask in the center of her warmth. Fynlee was one of the sweetest, most caring people he'd ever met. The man who won her heart would be fortunate and blessed.

The thought of anyone loving Fynlee, of knowing her love, made his smile dissolve and a scowl take its place. Aware that his feelings made no sense, it didn't change the fact that he didn't want anyone getting close to Fynlee.

Anyone except him.

The realization brought him up short. With perfect clarity, he finally knew exactly what he wanted.

Intent on reaching Fynlee, Carson moved through the crowd, barely acknowledging questions or comments tossed his way. When he finally stood beside her, he took the serving spoon out of her hand and she turned to look at him.

"What do you need, Carson?" she asked, looking up at him with a smile.

You.

At least that's what he wanted to say. Instead, he cleared his throat and waved a hand over the food table. "Most everyone has been through the line. Get a plate and sit with me," he said. Maybe he just needed to eat something. He skipped lunch and breakfast was a distant memory. Hunger could be the reason he felt so strange and couldn't keep his thoughts together — or at least from obsessing about Fynlee and how much he wanted to kiss her. He didn't have any problem fixating on those ideas.

Any sane man would have more than a passing interest in tasting those rich red lips of hers, wouldn't he?

Aggravated with himself and the continual direction of his thoughts, Carson handed Fynlee a plate and took one for himself. She poured cups of punch and followed him to two chairs at a table with some of the Golden Skies residents. Carson ate quietly while Fynlee laughed and teased those at their table.

Once everyone had eaten their fill, he signaled to the band to start playing music. They pushed several tables out of the way to create more room on the dance floor then encouraged everyone to get up and dance.

When no one seemed willing to be the first, Carson grabbed Fynlee's hand. "Someone needs to break the ice, so let's go."

She pulled back. "I don't think it needs to be me. I'm not a very good dancer."

He placed both hands beneath her arms and lifted her to her feet. "I'm not buying that. Come on. It'll be fun."

While he tugged her toward the dance floor, Fynlee offered a dozen reasons why he should choose a different dance partner. He ignored them all.

When they reached the open floor space, the band switched to a slower-paced song. Carson bowed to Fynlee, making her smile. He took her hand in his and led her in a dance. They'd circled the floor once then twice before several other couples joined them, some young, some old — but all ready to dance.

Throughout the evening, Carson snagged Fynlee as a partner several times. He also danced with every female resident of Golden Skies who attended the party, including Ruth.

To make a special memory for his aunt's friend, he asked the band to play *Waltzing Matilda* and spun Matilda Dale around the dance floor.

Fynlee grabbed her phone out of her pocket and snapped photos of them, laughing at the unforgettable spectacle the two of them made.

The band played one of Carson's favorite slow songs. He looked around and spied Fynlee laughing at something her grandmother said. A few long strides took him to her side.

"Dance with me, Rosie Red?"

"Why not? You've most likely recovered from

the last two times I stomped on your toes out there." Fynlee took his hand and followed him to the dance floor.

Somewhere between the second verse and the chorus, Carson settled both hands at her waist while her fingers wound around the back of his neck. Subtly, they inched closer to each other.

Oblivious to anyone else in the barn, their eyes met while their hearts connected. Carson pulled her even closer and she sighed contentedly.

Unbeknownst to them, Matilda and Ruth made a beeline for the band the moment they started dancing and insisted the song continue. The band played it two more times while the meddling matchmakers watched their plans for Carson and Fynlee to fall in love begin to settle into place.

They held hands and their breath as Carson dipped his head to Fynlee's, about to kiss her. A lazy grin spread across his face and blue flames smoldered in his eyes as his mouth descended toward hers.

Ruth had to shush Matilda to keep her from squealing in excitement when Carson's mouth hovered a breath of space above Fynlee's.

At that precise moment, a shrill, grating voice rang through the barn, sounding more like the screech of metal on a train as it ground to a halt than a noise generated by a human.

A petite blonde bombshell entered the barn in a cloud of expensive perfume. Her presence instantly derailed all of Matilda and Ruth's plans for a romance between Carson and Fynlee.

"Car-Car! I'm here!" Hilary shouted above the

music of the band and noise of the crowd.

The band stopped playing and every eye in the barn turned to watch as Hilary teetered her way through the partygoers to where Carson stood with Fynlee.

The disruptive sound of her voice caused him to lift his head and move away from Fynlee just before their mouths touched. Even with a separation of space, he hadn't completely cleared the fire from his eyes or the itch from his lips to taste Fynlee's.

Astounded by what had almost happened in front of a barn full of witnesses, Fynlee stepped away from Carson.

An urge to spin on her heel and run out to her car almost propelled her out the door. Instead, she slowly backed away from the man she loved while the woman he loved approached on six-inch stilettos.

"Car-Car! Why didn't you tell me you were having a party? I would have arrived sooner." Hilary wrapped a possessive hand around his arm.

The smile she gave him made Fynlee think of a cat before it pounced on an unsuspecting bird.

Fynlee did her best not to judge the woman, but she took an instant dislike to her. From the blonde hair on her head to the manicured toes peeking out of her ridiculous shoes, everything about her seemed fake and laced with a hint of malice.

"Hey, Hilary. What a surprise," Carson said, clearly disappointed by her unexpected arrival. Without a speck of warmth or enthusiasm, he kissed her cheek. "Aunt Ruth and Mrs. Dale organized this party. Isn't it great?"

"I'm sure it's quite nice for a country bumpkin celebration." Hilary sneered at Fynlee. "At least I assume that was the intended theme."

Carson ignored her comment and held a hand out toward Fynlee. "This is Fynlee Dale. She helped me get ready for the party and is a good friend."

"How good?" Hilary narrowed her calculating gaze, and lowered her mask for the briefest moment.

What Fynlee saw made a cold shiver slither down her spine. Perhaps it was wiser to compare Hilary to a snake before it struck its prey.

Hilary yanked on Carson's arm, demanding he get her something to eat and drink. He gave Fynlee one more look before leading Hilary off the dance floor. Although he suggested she fix a plate from the food left in the barn, she insisted he take her to the house.

When they left, the party quietly ended. Parents gathered their children. Fynlee helped Sage load the residents heading back to Golden Skies on the bus while the band packed up their instruments.

Matilda and Ruth, along with some of Fynlee's friends, started filling garbage bags with trash.

"We can finish the rest tomorrow," Ruth said, wrapping an arm around Fynlee's waist and giving it a squeeze. "Why don't Tillie and I catch a ride with Sage, then you won't have to go out of your way to drop us off."

"I don't mind," Fynlee said, hugging Ruth.

Matilda wrapped her arms around Fynlee from behind, sandwiching her between the two older women. "I know you don't, sweet girl, but you're tired and the last thing you need is to take us two old biddies home. We'll see you in the morning for church."

"Okay," Fynlee said, too weary to argue. She walked Ruth and her grandmother to the activity bus and watched them climb onboard. Once they were seated, she waved at Sage.

She thanked her friends who'd helped clean up and bid them goodnight as they headed out to their cars.

In desperate need of a good cry, she shoved her emotions aside and tapped on the kitchen door. Reluctantly, she stuck her head inside the house. Hilary clung to Carson with her body practically wrapped around him. For all appearances, they shared a very intimate kiss.

Stunned, Fynlee turned to escape, but Carson pushed Hilary aside and stepped Fynlee's direction. For a moment, he looked dismayed, and she wasn't sure if it was because she'd caught him in a lover's embrace with Hilary or because he'd almost kissed her earlier.

He took another step closer to her. "I'm sorry, Fynlee. I meant to get out there earlier to help."

She held up a hand, hoping he wouldn't come any closer to her. "It's fine. We'll finish tomorrow, but there is some food left on the tables. You might want to bring it in or give it to your hired hands."

"I'll take care of it." Carson glanced down at the hand clutching his arm and pried Hilary's fingers loose. "I'll be right back, Hil."

"I'll come with you," she said, wrapping her fingers around his arm again and shooting a look at

Fynlee meant as a warning.

"You don't need to see me out. Good night." Fynlee turned and fled around the corner of the house. She almost tripped over Gus and Jack, forgetting Carson had left them in the fenced yard to keep them from getting underfoot.

She gave them both a hasty pat on the head before racing to her car. Tears burned her eyes and clogged her throat, but she managed to make it back to her apartment before collapsing on her bed and giving them release.

Convinced Carson had intended to kiss her during the slow dance, she considered if she'd imagined the whole thing. He'd held her close many times that evening. Told her repeatedly how great she looked. She thought she'd seen something in his eyes that went beyond friendly interest.

What had he planned to gain from boosting her ego? A fling?

He wasn't the type to engage in a meaningless affair and he had to know she'd never participate in one.

If Hilary hadn't shown up, would Carson really have kissed her? Would he have said he cared about her more than just as a friend?

All along, she'd known Carson had a girlfriend. Why, oh why, had she allowed herself to fall in love with him?

Chapter Six

"Is she still at the ranch?" Matilda asked, accepting the cup of tea Ruth held out to her.

"Unfortunately, yes." Ruth snapped her napkin open and draped it over her lap. Since the party Saturday, Hilary had taken up residence at the Flying B. It had been three days. Three very long days. "She's perfectly dreadful. I don't know what Carson was thinking to get involved with such a selfish, horrible young woman."

"She's beautiful. I'm sure that probably doesn't hurt anything. It sounds like her father has money to burn. From what you and Carson have said, I didn't think there were a lot of dating prospects where he grew up."

Ruth sighed. "That's true. But she's so manipulative and she uses Carson's good-nature and gentle heart to her advantage."

"Yes, she does." Matilda didn't believe in

hating anyone, but she loathed Hilary. The two times she'd endured her presence, she barely controlled her urge to slap the haughtiness right out of the girl.

"How's Fynlee?" Ruth had noticed the pain in her eyes the moment Hilary walked into the barn. It was obvious to everyone except her thick-skulled nephew that Fynlee was in love with him. From the scathing glares Hilary tossed at Fynlee, it seemed even she was aware of the attraction.

"Quiet. Sad." Matilda sipped her tea. "I tried to talk to her, but she muttered some nonsense about not wanting to discuss her stupidity."

Ruth appeared appalled. "Surely, she doesn't think falling in love with Carson was stupid."

Matilda nodded. "That's the idea I took away from our chat. I love that boy like he was my own, Ruthie, but I could just smack him into next week for being so dense. What is he thinking, letting that nasty woman stay at the ranch when he could be falling in love with Fynlee?"

"If you want to pop him one, you'll have to get in line behind me. The question is, Tillie, what are we going to do to fix this. We both know Hilary won't make him happy. I don't care what that woman says, Carson won't marry her. Not ever. I haven't yet figured out what she's after, but she doesn't love Carson."

Matilda snorted. "It would be hard for her to love anyone when she's so fixated on herself."

Ruth smiled. "That is true. At least she'll be gone after tomorrow. Carson called to confirm the time for my doctor appointment next week and said

Hilary was heading home in the morning. He sounded relieved."

"It's about time she left. I hope her broom runs out of gas on the way there." Matilda pushed her round glasses up on her nose and sniffed with an exaggerated measure of disdain.

Ruth reached over and gave Matilda a playful shove. "You better hope to goodness it doesn't. She'll call Carson to come to her rescue." Ruth shook her head, making her silver curls bounce. "No, we just need her to be long gone and never return."

"Okay. With her out of sight, let's hope she'll also be out of mind. Did you see how close Carson was to kissing our girl during the dance?" Matilda's face took on a wistful expression.

"So close I bet he's kicking himself for hesitating." Ruth grinned then sipped her tea.

Matilda sighed. "I could be wrong, but Carson didn't look happy Hilary showed up. He appeared perfectly miserable when she came into town with him Sunday for church. Why doesn't he tell her to get lost?"

A shrug lifted Ruth's round shoulders. "I have no idea. Regardless of what he says or how much he tries to convince himself he owes Hilary his loyalty, he has his eye on Fynlee. I think it's so adorable, the way he calls her Rosie Red."

"She hated to be called Rosie growing up, but she practically melts when Carson says it."

"It's true love, I tell you!" Ruth smacked the table with her hand in an uncharacteristic show of boldness. "I don't care if we have to lock them in a room until they both come to their senses or scrabble together sufficient funds to send Hilary on a slow boat to China, but we have to do something."

"And we will, Ruthie. Pass me a piece of that delicious banana bread you baked yesterday and let's figure this out."

Chapter Seven

"Fynlee? Hey, Fynlee!" Carson jogged to catch up to her as she left work and hurried across the frosty parking lot toward her car.

Since the disastrous arrival of Hilary at the harvest party, Fynlee had avoided him. He'd tried to talk to her at church, but she somehow managed to evade him, making sure she kept her grandmother and his aunt between them at all times.

He'd texted her but received no replies.

Despite the clarity he'd gained that evening about what and who he really wanted, he'd made a mess of things. Out of loyalty or kindness, or maybe the part of him that hated to deal with crying women, he'd not said anything to Hilary in October about breaking up with her.

He'd saved that conversation for Thanksgiving when he spent the holiday with his parents and brothers.

The trip home for Thanksgiving gave him plenty of time to get his thoughts in order. For the first time, he saw the way Hilary looked down her nose at his family and noticed how she tried to manipulate both him and his time.

Relief mingled with a bit of self-loathing when he sat down with Hilary and explained he no longer wanted to date her.

Almost immediately, her perky mask slipped away, replaced by a bitter, jealous monster. She fumed and cried, threw things at him, and refused to listen.

Hastily leaving before she improved her aim and did him bodily harm, he followed up with a phone call a few hours later. That resulted in more shrieking and crying. She screeched that he needed time to realize he would marry her then hung up.

Hilary was so, so wrong.

The only thing he needed was to figure out a way to get Fynlee to talk to him again.

Focused on that particular goal, little else seemed important. Even if nothing came of it beyond restoring the friendship they'd enjoyed, Carson could live with that. What he couldn't live without was the sound of Fynlee's laughter and the sight of her smile.

He'd missed her so much in the past month and refused to go another day without making an effort to set things right between them. That's why he'd gone to the hospital and sat outside in the cold, waiting for her to leave for the day.

As she cast him a wary glance and continued walking, he knew he had his work cut out for him.

"Fynlee, will you please talk to me?" He reached out and caught her arm, gently pulling her to a stop.

"I don't think there's anything to say, Carson. Or should I call you Car-Car?" At the annoyed look on his face, she tugged her arm free of his grasp. "That's the nickname you hated, isn't it?"

He nodded his head. "Yeah, it is." With a weary sigh, he removed his hat and ran a hand over his head before settling it back in place. "Please, Fynlee. I'm sorry for what happened at the party. I know Hilary was rude to you, on top of everything else."

She took a few steps away from him. The last thing she wanted was to rehash that horrible evening.

"Will you please talk to me?" He followed her as she walked over to her car.

"I don't think that's a good idea, Carson. You aren't the only one to blame. I shouldn't have… it was…" Fynlee unlocked her car and set her purse inside. "It's fine. I'm not mad at you or anything." And she wasn't. The angry feelings burning her from the inside out began with herself for ever giving Carson a second glance and ended with horrid Hilary.

"Well, that's good to know. The way you've been avoiding me kind of gave me the idea you hated my guts."

The barest hint of a smile touched Fynlee's lips. "I would never hate your guts. If I was going to hate something, it would be your big head or that thick neck that looks like a tree trunk or that hideously ugly face of yours or maybe…"

Carson smirked and held his hands up in front of him, as if to ward off her words. "I get it. Enough."

She grinned and rubbed her hands together to dispel the cold, trying to recall what she'd done with her gloves.

"Please, Fynlee. Would you have dinner with me? There's something important I want to talk to you about."

At the pleading look on his face and the hopeful spark in his eye, she sighed. "Okay. But I need to run by and check on Grams first."

"I just came from there. She and Aunt Ruth were playing a rousing game of cards when I left. Matilda said to give you this." Carson removed a folded piece of paper from his coat pocket and handed it to her.

Fynlee took the note and read it, rolled her eyes, and stuffed it into her pocket. "It appears I've been banned from setting foot at the Hokey Pokey Hotel this evening."

"Perfect. You are officially out of excuses not to eat dinner with me." He appeared ready to beg if she refused again.

With an exasperated sigh, she agreed. "Fine. But I'm driving myself and paying for my own meal. Where should I meet you?"

"The diner?" Carson suggested. The food was good and it typically wasn't too busy on a weeknight, affording them a measure of privacy.

"The diner it is. I'll meet you there in a minute." Fynlee started her car and waited for the heater to kick on before she backed out of her parking space and drove to the diner.

Although she'd seen Carson at church and at Golden Skies a few times, she'd nearly forgotten how handsome he was up close, how good he smelled.

Merciful stars! How was she supposed to pretend she wasn't interested in him when he flashed that killer smile or gave her that boyish, encouraging look?

Ruth had mentioned in passing that Carson had taken a break from Hilary, but a break didn't mean he'd told her good riddance and goodbye. Until that happened, Fynlee was safeguarding her heart and not getting any more involved with the hunky cowboy.

She wanted to be angry with him for paying any attention to Hilary. It was beyond her ability to understand how he could be around someone so shallow, but Hilary was a looker.

If Carson's type of girl was petite, blonde, and needy, Fynlee was about as opposite as he could find. Tall, dark-haired and independent, she was used to taking care of herself as well as others.

She parked the car at the diner, half-dreading whatever Carson had to say to her. Recalling their near-kiss at the party made her defensive. It wasn't like they'd done anything wrong.

However, if Hilary had waited two more seconds for her obnoxious entrance, she would have found them with their lips locked together.

Fynlee wasn't surprised when Carson opened her door and offered her his hand. With a slight hesitation, she took it and slid out of the car. When she tried to pull her hand free of his grasp, he grinned at her. "It looks like it might be slick. You better hang on, just to be safe."

The prolonged contact of their fingers was about as far from safe as Fynlee could imagine, but she wisely kept her thoughts to herself.

Inside the diner, they found a seat at a corner booth at the back. Carson helped remove her coat before taking off his and tossing his black Stetson on the seat beside him.

"I'm curious to hear what was so important you hunted me down at work and got me kicked out of Golden Skies for the evening?" Fynlee asked, staring at him.

"All in good time, my friend. First, let's order something to eat. I'm starving." Carson smiled at the waitress as she handed them menus and set down glasses of ice water.

After they'd placed orders and Fynlee held a cup of hot tea between her cold hands, Carson took several papers from his coat pocket, unfolded them, and slid them across the table.

"What's this?" Fynlee asked, sipping her tea.

Carson tapped his finger on the top sheet. "I did a little research on occupational therapists."

Uncertain what to make of his sudden interest in her choice of career, she eyed him apprehensively. "And you did that because…?"

"Because I wanted to know more about what it was you studied to do, what you could do." He shuffled through the papers and set one in front of her with a list of possible career options. "Are you dead set on working with kids?"

"Not necessarily. It was my first choice, but I'd work with rabid dogs at this point just to be able to get into the field."

Carson shot her the lopsided smirk she loved seeing on his handsome face.

He tapped a finger on the page in front of her. "I don't think anything that drastic will be necessary. However, if you're willing to work with the elderly, I know a certain retirement village that has a job opening up in January."

Fynlee's head snapped up and she leaned toward Carson. "You are kidding me, right? This is some sick joke meant to completely break my heart."

"Rosie Red, I'd never, ever break your heart," Carson said, taking her hand in his and giving it a squeeze. "I had a meeting with the facility manager earlier today. The topic of therapy happened to come up and one thing led to another. Mrs. Romans wasn't aware of your degree. She said she'd like you to set up a time to speak with her about the position. When I mentioned it to your grandmother, she said you've been doing volunteer therapy work at the hospital."

Fynlee shrugged. "It's no big deal. I enjoy helping others and it gives me something to do on my lunch break rather than sit around and wait for an hour to pass. It also keeps my training up-to-date." The impact of what Carson had done for her, the door he'd cracked open into a possibility for her career, hit her with full force.

Suddenly drained, she leaned back in the booth

and dabbed at her eyes with a paper napkin.

"What's wrong?" he asked, unsettled by her tears.

"It's just so nice of you to do this." She brushed away a few teardrops that spilled down her cheeks.

"I didn't do anything. You're the one who'll have to dazzle Mrs. Romans, but at least you know there are a few job opportunities out there."

"But why do you care?" Fynlee swiped at her nose and looked at Carson with eyes that shimmered from the moisture gathering in them.

"Because you're my friend, that's why. I've really missed you, Fynlee, missed your friendship. Hilary was a pill at the harvest party, but I don't want that to keep us from being friends. Your friendship is important to me, much more so than you realize. I'm sorry for whatever happened that evening to make you think otherwise."

Fynlee nodded. She didn't possess the self-will or strength to deny him her friendship. She enjoyed being around him too much.

The past weeks had been painfully dull and lonesome, even with Matilda and Ruth doing their best to keep things lively.

"Great. Now, I want to hear all about the crazy stuff your grandmother has done that she and Aunt Ruth refuse to tell me about. I heard from Sage at the front desk that Matilda showed up for Thanksgiving dinner wearing a feathered headdress and buckskins."

"She sure did." Fynlee smiled and relaxed, grateful to be back on steady footing with Carson. "I have no idea where she got that outfit, but she wore it all day. It was almost as good as her Halloween costume."

Chapter Eight

"Carson? Are you here?" Fynlee called as she entered the warmth of his shop. He'd asked her to come out to the ranch to help him decorate for Christmas. He wanted to surprise Ruth by having the decorations up when she came to visit after church on Sunday.

Matilda and Fynlee were included in the invitation and looked forward to spending the afternoon at the ranch.

Today, though, Fynlee had been almost to the ranch when she received a text from Carson asking her to meet him in his shop.

Before the harvest party, she'd been in the building a few times and knew where to find it.

After parking her car at the house, she cut through the yard and out the side gate. Snow fell in big, fluffy flakes around her and she turned her face up, catching several on her tongue.

Gus and Jack yipped and raced over to her, bumping into her legs and begging for attention.

She stopped to pet them before continuing on to the shop. As she opened the door and stepped inside, the smell of diesel mingled with cedar and varnish.

"Carson?"

He stepped out from behind a partition and smiled at her. "Hey, Rosie Red. Come over here and let me know what you think."

She skirted around the space heater that warmed the shop and a tractor in the midst of repairs to a workbench where Carson sat on a high stool.

"What are you doing?" she asked, eyeing the sawdust and tools around him.

"Making a little present for Aunt Ruth for Christmas." Carson bent over and blew a few wood shavings away from a wooden daisy he'd just carved.

"Oh, my goodness! You made that?" Fynlee leaned closer to study the intricately carved wooden basket full of blooms that appeared so realistic she could almost smell their fragrance.

Carson smiled, pleased by her reaction to his efforts. "Yeah. I do a little woodworking when I have time. It's just a fun hobby."

"This is amazing and Ruth will adore it." Fynlee beamed at him as she ran a finger over a delicate rose. "I've heard her mention how much she missed the flowers here, and now you're giving them back to her."

"I hope she'll like it. I'm putting a hook on the

back so she can hang it on the wall." Carson wiped off his hands and draped a cloth over the carving and his tools. When he rose to his feet, he brushed against Fynlee and she took a quick step back. "So, are you ready to help me deck the halls?"

A grin tickled the corners of her mouth. "Lead on, Mr. Ford. Let's make your holly all jolly."

Three hours later, Carson plopped down on the couch and settled into the cushions. "I'm done, Rosie Red. Done being your decorating slave. Done decking the halls. Done in and absolutely all done."

Fynlee giggled and sat beside him. "Drink this, and then you'll be ready for round two."

Carson turned his head and gave her a doubtful glare as he accepted the cup of hot chocolate she held out to him.

When their fingers touched, she dropped her hand as soon as he accepted the mug. She slid further down the couch, away from him and the temptation he presented.

Relaxed against the couch cushions, he appeared both boyish and ruggedly appealing. His hair was a tousled mess and scruff covered his cheeks.

The impulse to reach out and run her hand along that strong jaw and into his thick hair was so strong, she wrapped her fingers around the mug of chocolate to keep from doing something she'd regret.

They were just getting back to the casual, relaxed friendship they'd shared before the harvest party. She didn't want anything to mess it up.

Even if she'd never own Carson's heart,

maintaining their friendship was important to her. She realized she would rather have that relationship with him than none at all.

For his part, Carson had been entertaining and attentive to her as they decorated the house, telling her things he remembered from the one Christmas he spent at the farm as a boy. Like now, he recalled things he'd enjoyed from past Christmases.

"Aunt Ruth used to make this peanut butter candy that was so good. Sometimes she'd mail us a box. I wonder if she still has the recipe." Carson took a sip of his hot chocolate and stared into the flames of the fire he'd built earlier.

It crackled and cast amber light around the room.

A romantic glow, Fynlee mused, if she was inclined to consider such things, which she most certainly was not.

"Why don't you ask her?" she suggested, stretching out her long legs and resting her feet on the coffee table in front of them.

"I'll do that." Carson was quiet for a long moment then looked at Fynlee again. "What about you? Do you have any special memories from Christmases with Matilda?"

"Christmas was never very traditional with Grams. Oh, we'd put up a tree, but the decorations changed every year, depending on what theme she was into at the time. One year, she decided we could only decorate with pine cones and peacock feathers."

Carson shook his head, trying to picture a tree bedecked with peacock feathers. "That must have been interesting."

"It was," Fynlee smiled, recalling some of the crazy, yet memorable Christmas celebrations she had with her grandparents. "Gramps was nothing like Grams, you know, but he always encouraged her to do whatever she liked."

"I think it's nice he loved her that much, to accept who she was and encourage it."

Fynlee nodded. "They had a special relationship. I sure miss him and I know Grams does, too. I sometimes think she does such zany stuff because it reminds her of good times with Gramps."

"Possibly. Your grandmother seems to get a kick out of challenging people, challenging their ideas of what's acceptable. That's not necessarily a bad thing."

Fynlee sipped her chocolate. "She does. The presence of your aunt has helped, though. Grams hasn't done anything eye-rolling outlandish for a while."

"Does that mean she's plotting a doozy or mellowing in her old age?"

She shrugged. "It could go either way." After another long sip of her chocolate, she set down the mug and got to her feet. "Come on. We still need to finish hanging the lights outside."

"I'll do it later," he said, growing drowsy in the heat from the fire and the comfortable companionship Fynlee provided. Her presence there, helping him decorate, felt so right, like she belonged on the Flying B with him.

As his thoughts spun off in the direction of his

future, he clasped Fynlee's hand in his and tried to pull her down on the couch beside him.

The kiss that never happened at the harvest party had left him even more determined to explore the possibility of a relationship with her.

The sizzle between them was something he could feel from his head to his toes every time their skin made even the slightest contact. That attraction kept him awake at night, dreaming of making her his own.

He'd never felt anything even remotely like it with Hilary and somewhere in his heart, Carson knew he'd never experience it with anyone else. In truth, he didn't want to feel it with anyone else.

Only Fynlee.

She was sweet and kind, giving and fun, dedicated and intelligent. He couldn't think of anything he didn't like about the girl, even her loony grandmother. He adored her freckles and smile, the way her eyes lit from within, and the expressive openness of her face.

The fact she had no idea how pretty she was only left him even more attracted to her.

Carson had fallen for her, but he wasn't sure she felt the same. After the debacle with Hilary before Halloween, he knew it would take some time to approach Fynlee not as a friend, but as a man who was crazy in love with her.

Fynlee's voice cut into his ponderings, drawing him back to the present. "If you're going to be a lazy bones and spend the rest of the evening here, I'm heading home."

"You're such a party pooper, Rosie Red."

Carson banked his yearning for her and rose to his feet, following her to the kitchen where they'd left boxes of outdoor lights to string along the eves of the house.

Carson tamped his feet into winter boots and pulled on his coat then opened the door to carry the boxes outside. Snow blew with such force, he could barely see the edge of the fence around the yard.

"Fynlee?"

"I'm coming," she said, rushing up behind him then sucking in her breath. "My goodness, I better hit the road if I want to get home tonight."

He shook his head and set down the box of lights in his hand. "You aren't going anywhere in that little car of yours. Tonight, you'll stay here."

Fynlee glared at him as if he'd uttered complete nonsense. "Are you insane? I'm not spending the night here. If Grams and Ruth found out, there'd be a shotgun wedding in your immediate future."

Carson gave her a devilish smile and sidled closer to her. "I'd be okay with that. You'd make a beautiful bride. Do you think they'd give us time to plan a wedding or would they round up a gun and march us right over to the church? Maybe we can convince them to hold off until Valentine's Day. You can't get too much more romantic than that."

She smacked his chest with her mitten-covered hand. "Stop teasing me. I really do need to go."

"I wasn't teasing about the wedding or the weather." Carson unzipped his coat and closed the door. "You aren't driving home in this."

Fynlee grabbed his zipper and pulled it upward. "Then you'll just have to drive me home in that big ol' pickup of yours."

Carson kicked off his boots. "Are you trying to get us both killed? It would be foolhardy and dangerous to head out in a storm like this. Before long, you won't be able to see more than a foot or two in front of you." He unzipped his coat and hung it up on a peg by the door before Fynlee could zip it up again.

"Take off your coat and stay awhile, because you aren't leaving until morning." He tugged off her red mittens and the red knit cap on her head. She looked so cute with the hat making static electricity dance through her dark hair, he almost surrendered to his need to kiss her.

Once he started kissing her, though, he wouldn't be able to stop. That was an indisputable fact. Instead of giving in to his desire, he took a step back.

A long night of keeping his hands and lips to himself loomed ahead of him, so he strolled over to the refrigerator, seeking a distraction.

He heard her sigh and listened to the thud of her boots hitting the floor as she removed them. "I've got some leftover chicken casserole or I can make sandwiches. What's your preference?"

"To go home," Fynlee said, taking a seat on a barstool at the counter. "Since you've removed that option from the table, casserole will be fine. What can I do to help?"

Carson grinned and tossed her a head of lettuce. "Make a salad."

After they ate, Carson bundled up to go check on the stock outside and to make sure the dogs and his crew were doing fine.

To pass the time, Fynlee made popcorn and they munched it while drinking more hot chocolate and watching old movies. When neither of them could keep their eyes open any longer, Carson led the way upstairs to a guestroom.

"This one has a private bath. If you get cold, there are extra blankets in the closet." He turned and disappeared down the hall then quickly returned with one of his T-shirts. "This might work for a sleep shirt since you don't have anything else."

"Thanks, Carson. I'll see you in the morning."

"You bet, Rosie Red. Sleep well and if you need anything, let me know."

At her curt nod, he stepped into the hall and closed the door, wishing she'd give him some indication that she'd welcome his affection.

Then again, it was probably best a bit of frost edged between the two of them. Otherwise, he might not be able to stay out of her room. As it was, he wanted to walk inside the bedroom and take her in his arms, hold her all night.

A vision of Fynlee with her luxurious black hair spilling over her pillow made him swallow hard. Her fragrance lingered in the hall, so he hurried to his room and took a shower.

After spending hours tossing and turning, Carson finally fell asleep, but awoke early. He dressed then quietly made his way down the back stairs. In the kitchen, he looked outside at the blanket of snow. At least the whiteout conditions had passed, even if it was bitterly cold outside.

As soon as the snowplows cleared the highway,

he'd drive Fynlee into town. Her car wasn't going anywhere until he dug it out. It wasn't safe for her to drive it today, anyway.

He started a pot of coffee then bundled into his chore clothes and made his way out to the barn. The dogs greeted him as he stepped inside. After checking with his hired hands and helping with the feeding, he returned inside to find Fynlee at the stove flipping pancakes.

The sight of her in his kitchen, making him breakfast, gave him a glimpse of what he wanted to see every morning.

Fynlee.

With her dark hair falling in waves down her back and freckles dancing across her nose and cheeks, he drank in the sight of her. Tall and graceful, he loved watching the easy way she moved.

The deep breath he inhaled filled his nose with more than the aroma of breakfast. Her decadent scent infused the air, making him want things he had no right even to imagine. Not yet, anyway.

"Morning, Rosie Red." Carson tried to hide his fascination with her behind a teasing smile.

"Good morning. The smell of the coffee drew me down here. Hope you don't mind, but I already had a cup."

"Nope. As long as you left a little for me, you can have all you want." Carson poured a mug full then took a long sip. "You didn't have to cook breakfast."

"I wanted to. It's not much. I'm hoping to coerce you into taking me to town. I know it's pointless to beg you to let me drive myself."

"You've got that right." Carson grinned and took another drink of his coffee. "And if you think you need to rush to get to church, the parson called and said the roads are so bad, they've canceled services this morning."

"Oh. At least we won't have to worry about taking Grams and Ruth out in this." Fynlee poured more batter into the skillet.

Carson shook his head. "I wouldn't have taken them anyway. What if one of the ol' gals slipped and broke something? I don't want that on my head."

Fynlee smiled. "Like they'd have given you a choice. If they decide to do something, it would take more than your refusal to change their mind."

The point she made was one he couldn't argue. "True."

As she flipped the last pancake out of the skillet, Fynlee pointed to a platter of bacon. "Let's eat then go check on Grams and Ruth."

After breakfast, Fynlee did the dishes and set the kitchen to rights while Carson went out to start his truck. It took him a while to remove all the snow and get the door open.

When he drove it up to the end of the front walk, Fynlee rushed outside, antsy to leave. No matter how hard she tried to convince Carson she needed to return to town to check on Grams, the truth was that she couldn't spend one more minute in the house. Not when being there with him felt so wonderfully right, like she belonged there.

Last night, when he'd brought her one of his T-shirts to wear, she wanted to kiss him so badly that her lips still ached from the yearning. She spent most of the night snuggled into that shirt, wishing it were Carson's arms wrapped around her instead.

The shirt smelled of him, of his earthy, manly scent. Desperately, she wanted to take it with her, to have it to cuddle with every night, but she left it on the end of the guest bed.

Determined to let go of her silly dreams, she trudged through the snow, ignoring Carson's hasty attempts to shovel a path for her. He gave up and tossed the shovel in the back of his pickup then rushed to open the passenger door.

She accepted his hand with a nod and climbed inside, knocking the snow from her boots before Carson shut the door.

On the way to town, she remained quiet, breathing shallowly to avoid inhaling Carson's inviting scent. With her self-control at the breaking point, she needed space and time away from the temptation he unwittingly presented. If she didn't leave his enthralling presence soon, she might do something completely irrational like confess her love for him or ravage him with kisses.

Amused by the picture in her mind of the stunned look on his face if she were to be so forward, she forced herself to focus on the world outside the pickup window.

The plows had been out. While much of the snow had been removed, what remained made traveling slick and hazardous. Fynlee counted five cars off the road on the short drive to town.

Grateful for Carson's safe driving and his big

pickup, she breathed a sigh of relief when he pulled up at Golden Skies.

"I figured you'd want to see your grandmother before I take you home."

"I can walk home later. It's not that far," she said, hopping out of the truck before Carson made it around to open her door.

They'd barely set foot inside, when Matilda and Ruth rushed up and gave them both hugs. "Ruth and I were worried when Fynlee called to say you were driving her over. It was nice of you to pick her up and bring her."

Fynlee didn't set her grandmother straight. It was best she and Ruth had no idea about the snowstorm leaving her trapped at the ranch overnight.

Even though it was all innocent and nothing happened, not even a single kiss, the two old romantics would surely make something of it.

"Have you had breakfast?" Ruth asked as she looped her arm around Carson's.

"Yes, ma'am. I had a plate full of pancakes this morning that were better than usual." Carson winked at Fynlee and followed his aunt down the hall to the elevator.

A blush colored her cheeks every bit at as red as the nickname Carson had bestowed upon her.

"Are you okay, honey?" Matilda placed the back of her hand against Fynlee's forehead. "You aren't coming down with a cold are you? You look flushed."

"No, Grams. I'm fine." Fynlee scrambled to draw Matilda's attention away from her and onto something else. "Is there anything you'd like to do today?"

"Actually, if you wouldn't mind…"

Hours later, Fynlee had helped her grandmother address all her Christmas cards. In addition, she'd assisted in baking three batches of cookies and wrapped gifts Grams wanted to give to the staff at the retirement village. After she kissed her grandmother's cheek, she left with a promise to call to check on her later.

As she rushed off the elevator near the lobby, she ran into a solid chest. A familiar, undeniably seductive scent settled around her and she lifted her gaze. Carson's warm blue eyes twinkled with humor as he reached out to steady her.

"Hey, stranger." He released his hold and took a step back.

"Hey yourself," she said, unable to keep from smiling at him in return.

The keys to her car dangled from his fingers. "I thought you might like these."

"My keys?" she glanced at him in confusion.

"Yeah. I had the guys shovel out your car then I drove it into town. Tug is waiting for me outside, but I didn't want you to have to walk anywhere in this cold."

"Oh, gosh, Carson. That's so thoughtful. Thank you." Fynlee gave him an impulsive hug and immediately regretted it when she had to force herself to let go and step away from him.

"You're welcome." He walked her outside and over to where he'd parked her car close to the door. "Just be careful. Your car isn't made for icy roads."

"I know. It's a good thing I don't have far to drive." Fynlee opened her door and slid behind the wheel. "Thanks again, Carson."

"Anytime." He turned and started to walk away then glanced back at her. "Don't forget, you and Matilda are joining Aunt Ruth and me for Christmas Eve dinner at my house."

Fynlee nodded in agreement. "I didn't forget. We'll be there."

Chapter Nine

"That might have been the best turkey I've ever eaten, Carson," Matilda said, giving him a gracious smile.

"I'm glad you enjoyed it." Carson leaned back in his chair, content and full. The meal had been even better than he hoped. That morning, he'd picked up Ruth and brought her back to the ranch to spend the day with him. While he cooked the turkey in a slow cooker, Ruth made rolls and dressing along with citrus-laced cranberry sauce.

Matilda brought mashed potatoes and a broccoli dish smothered in cheese while Fynlee handled dessert, baking pumpkin and apple pies.

Carson sampled a slice of each. "The vote is still out on those pies, Rosie Red. They were both delicious, but I need to wait awhile and try them again, to be able to declare a favorite." A teasing wink made her blush as he turned his attention to the older women seated at the table. "You ladies all outdid yourselves. That was a fine meal."

"It certainly was," Ruth said, dabbing her mouth with a cheery red napkin. Without any urging on her part, Carson had used her holiday linens. When he'd shown her all the decorations he'd set out with Fynlee's help, she'd dabbed at her tears, pleased he treasured the things that had meant so much to her over the years.

Ruth glanced at Matilda and shared a conspiratorial smile. While Fynlee had gone outside with Carson to feed the dogs and check on the stock he'd fed earlier, the two older women managed to tack mistletoe all over the house.

"Why don't you two sit by the fire in the living room while we do the dishes?" Fynlee suggested to Ruth and Matilda, getting to her feet and carrying dishes to the sink.

"I think that's a grand idea," Ruth said, sliding back her chair and motioning for Matilda to join her. "My old bones sure do enjoy that cheery fire."

"Mine, too," Matilda said, following her friend into the front room.

Once there, they quietly sat on the couch and listened to the conversation in the kitchen.

"Thank you again for inviting us to join you, Carson." Fynlee placed leftover turkey into resealable freezer bags.

"You're more than welcome. It is my pleasure to have you. Those pies were both so good, and Matilda did a great job with the mashed potatoes." Carson glanced at her over his shoulder as he placed dishes in the dishwasher.

Fynlee grinned at him. "I'd tell you what was in Gram's potatoes, but your arteries might clog on the spot. I don't think I'm up for a trip to the emergency room this evening."

Chuckles filled the kitchen as he flicked soap bubbles at her. Batting at them with her hand, she wrinkled her nose and laughed.

The two of them worked together in silence for a few minutes before her voice dropped to a whisper and she tipped her head toward the living room. "Are you going to give your aunt her gift tonight or in the morning?"

"In the morning. I talked Aunt Ruth into spending the night here. I thought she might appreciate waking up Christmas morning at the ranch, like she has so many years in the past. A minimal amount of coaxing was required to get her to agree." Carson glanced at her again. "We're both glad you and Matilda will spend the day with us, too."

"You're so good to your aunt, Carson. I know she really appreciates all you do. And I appreciate how kind you are to Grams." Fynlee stopped spooning leftovers into storage containers and gave him a soft look. "Despite what anyone might say, you're one of the good guys."

"Don't you forget it, Rosie Red."

Another soap bubble floated toward her and she

popped it with a giggle. Suddenly, she sobered. "I wanted to thank you again for setting the wheels in motion for my new job." The look she cast at him held sincere gratitude. "If you hadn't made that initial contact with Mrs. Romans, I wouldn't have known about the position opening up in January. I'm so excited to start working at Golden Skies. I'll be closer to Grams and I'll be doing something I love."

"I really didn't do anything, but you're welcome. The job was meant for you and you'll do great at it." Carson's smile reflected his pride in her for going after the job and getting it. "It's nice your friend Carrie offered to let you take this week off instead of finishing your final two weeks at the billing center."

"The billing office is so quiet and boring the week after Christmas, Carrie struggles to keep the staff from climbing the walls. It'll be nice to have a week to do whatever I want."

"Perhaps some of that time off will find you here at the ranch. The hill is prime for sledding and the pond is frozen deep enough for skating. That snowman we built yesterday really could use a friend or two."

"With a little more persuasion, I could pencil you in."

Suggestively, he waggled an eyebrow at her. "What kind of persuasion are we talking about, Miss Dale?"

Even though her heart skipped a beat at his flirtatious teasing, she frowned. "Not that kind, I assure you."

Carson laughed and finished the dishes while Fynlee placed the last of the leftovers in the refrigerator. As she wiped her hands on a dishtowel, she noticed mistletoe hanging above the sink.

"Are you planning to smooch your aunt?" she asked, pointing to the greenery hanging by a red ribbon.

He turned around and stared at the mistletoe. "If you want to place bets, I'll wager the two conniving women in the other room had something to do with that."

Fynlee took a step closer and pointed to the mistletoe. "How do you suppose they got it up there? I hate to think of one of them climbing up on a chair or stool. They could have broken a hip."

Carson looked around and noticed a bunch of mistletoe hanging in the hallway to the bathroom and more of it decorating the other doorways. "I'm not sure, but they were busy."

As Fynlee moved past him to look into the hall, Carson wrapped his arms around her and pulled her close. "It seems a shame to let their efforts go to waste."

Slowly, she leaned against his chest as her heart pounded in an erratic rhythm. After months of dreaming about it, wishing for it, she anticipated finally experiencing the wonder of Carson's kiss. "I suppose, in the spirit of a longstanding Christmas tradition, one kiss beneath the mistletoe wouldn't hurt."

"No, it wouldn't." Already focused on Fynlee's lips, his words came out in a husky mumble. Later, he'd have to remember to thank his aunt and

Matilda for hanging mistletoe everywhere. Now, though, he couldn't think of anything beyond finally tasting Fynlee's sweet lips.

He moved his hands up to bracket her face before his mouth brushed against hers in a tentative touch. When she didn't pull away, he deepened the kiss and wrapped her in his arms.

A blinding explosion of colorful lights danced behind his eyes and he could have sworn he heard chimes.

Nothing in his entire twenty-nine years of existence had ever felt as right as kissing Fynlee Rose Dale, right there in his kitchen with his aunt and her grandma spying on them from the other room.

If he'd wanted to stop kissing her, a thought that hadn't even blipped through his mind, he couldn't. The taste of her mouth, pure sweetness with a hint of pumpkin from the pie she'd eaten, became an addictive flavor he needed to savor over and over again.

The moment Fynlee slid her hands up his arms and laced them behind his neck, he lifted her off her feet and kissed her more thoroughly, more passionately than he'd ever imagined kissing anyone.

Breathless and holding onto his self-control by a thin thread, he lifted his head, wondering what reaction Fynlee would have to his ardent attention to her mouth.

The inviting sparkle in her eye and the flirty smile riding her lips chased away any lingering doubts he may have had about her feelings for him.

Encouraged, he fused his gaze to hers, eager to kiss her again.

As though she read his mind, she pointed to a sprig of greenery in the hall. "There's more mistletoe over there." The low sultry tone of her voice spiked his internal temperature and caused his ability for rational thought to dissipate.

"Let's test it out, too." He grinned as he swung her beneath the mistletoe and repeated the process of blending their lips in fervent kisses that, by some Christmas miracle, didn't set the entire kitchen aflame.

The kisses they shared were the most amazing gift he'd ever received. Greedily, he wanted more and more of them.

Whispers caught his attention as Ruth and Matilda tried to sneak out of the kitchen without being seen.

"We've been made." Carson grinned against Fynlee's mouth.

"So we have. No need to disappoint them now." The kiss she initiated created a new shower of sparks between the two of them. Carson quickly took control of it. Bells chimed again as they kissed until they both were out of breath.

Contentedly, he sighed, resting his forehead against hers. "You, my beautiful Christmas rose, are the sweetest, most wonderful present I've ever had. By now, you have to know…"

A banging sound at the patio door drew their gaze to Hilary as she stepped inside, stomping snow from her feet.

"Those two crazy old bats in the front room

slammed the door in my face and locked it. I had to trudge through the snow to the patio door," she said, removing her gloves and staring at Carson.

"What are you doing, Car-Car?" Hilary rushed over to him and yanked on his arm, pulling it away from where it rested around Fynlee's waist. "I flew out here to spend Christmas with you and endured a car trip from the airport with some redneck dunce, only to find you cheating on me with that… that… backwater nitwit!"

Carson stepped away from Fynlee, intent on removing Hilary from his home. "Look, Hilary, I don't know how to make it any clearer to you, but we're…"

"Getting married as soon as you take me home. Daddy has everything all arranged," Hilary said, flaunting a gaudy diamond in Fynlee's face. "If we leave in the morning, we can be Mr. and Mrs. Car-Car Ford before the end of the year." Hilary glowered at Fynlee. "You're not welcome here, miss whatever-your-name-is. Carson is mine and I don't share, especially not with the likes of you. It's time for you to go. When you leave, make sure you take those ghastly old women with you, too."

Astounded by Hilary's unexpected arrival and the fact she wore an engagement ring, Fynlee was too stunned to do more than back toward the living room. Ruth held a restraining hand on Matilda's arm to keep her from carrying through with her threat to slap Hilary all the way back to town.

"Did you not hear me? It's time for you to leave." Hilary made a shooing motion Fynlee's direction. "Are you stupid as well as homely?"

Carson grabbed Hilary's hand and started to walk her to the door. "The only one who's leaving is…"

Without warning, Hilary leaped at Carson, wrapping her legs around his waist and kissing him full on the mouth.

Shocked and disgusted, he tried to push her away without hurting her. Growing up in a house full of rough and tumble boys, his mother had made a point of ensuring all her sons were gentle around girls, afraid they might innocently hurt someone without realizing their own strength.

That restraint worked against Carson as he carefully attempted to dislodge Hilary. The more he pushed, the harder she held on, digging her nails into the back of his neck and crossing her ankles together around his waist.

Blindsided by the kiss and furious that she clawed his neck, Carson battled to free her hold. In a moment of panic, he placed one hand on her backside and lifted her upward while his other grabbed her fingers, desperate to be rid of her.

To the three onlookers, it appeared that he was fully engaged and willingly participating in the kiss, squirming against Hilary while moving his hands across her shoulders.

Ruth and Matilda both sucked in a huge gulp of air when Carson's hand settled on Hilary's little rump and he captured her fingers in something that resembled a lover's caress. The sound of Hilary's moan carried confirmation of their suspicions as it sliced through the silence of the room.

"My stars!" Ruth gasped, clutching a hand to

her chest.

Fynlee spun around and hurried to the door where she'd left her coat and boots. Matilda moved with a speed previously unexplored as she pulled on her outerwear.

When they turned to tell Ruth good night, she fastened the buttons on her coat and picked up her overnight bag. "Let's go."

None of them spoke as Fynlee helped the two women out to her car. She'd just closed Matilda's door when Carson ran outside in his socks, trying to get her to stop. "Fynlee! Don't leave. This is a big misunderstanding. Please come back inside!" he pleaded from the porch.

Hair rumpled from Hilary's hands running through it and smears of her garish red lipstick across his face only made matters worse.

Appalled, Fynlee gaped at him. The chance for him to explain evaporated the moment Hilary slunk behind him, wrapping her arms around his waist. The diamond on her finger glittered in the Christmas lights, like a two-carat slap to Fynlee's face.

More angry and hurt than she'd ever been in her life, Fynlee slid in the car, slammed the door, and drove down the driveway.

Carson turned on Hilary with a look of such rage, she hastily backed away from him, stumbling over the door's threshold and falling on the seat of her designer jeans.

"What part of the fact that I'm not interested in you is too hard for you to understand? I don't want to marry you, Hilary. I don't even want to be in the same room with you. How dare you show up on Christmas Eve with that ring on your finger? Did Daddy buy that for you, too?"

Hilary blanched as she worked to get to her feet in her high-heeled boots. "But Car-Car, I thought…"

Ice frosted his glare as he yanked on a coat and tamped his cold, wet feet into boots. "For the record, I hate the name Car-Car. I always have. I hate that I wasted so much time trying to convince myself I loved you. And I really hate that you just made the woman I love think I don't care about her."

He stormed into the kitchen and grabbed Hilary's suitcase and purse. The slam of the back door rattled behind him as he jogged out to his truck and pulled it out front.

It idled with the heater on high as he stalked up the front walk and grabbed Hilary by her arm, pulling her outside and down the steps.

The heels of her boots weren't meant for snowy, icy sidewalks. Cautiously, she picked her way down the walk then slipped on a hidden spot of ice. Before she could fall, she grasped Carson's coat to keep herself upright.

Out of patience with his uninvited guest, Carson hefted her beneath his arm with her head and feet dangling. Despite her vehement protests, he carried her like a sack of feed to his truck before depositing her in the backseat.

"You will not say a word while I drive into town or so help me, I'll leave you head-first in a snowbank." Carson's menacing stare was enough to make her snap her mouth shut and buckle her seatbelt.

The little airport in town didn't have any available flights until the following afternoon. The reasonable thing to do would have been to take Hilary to a hotel and leave her there.

However, reason had flown out of Carson's head a few seconds after Hilary called Fynlee a backwater nitwit.

Refusing to allow her to stay in town, he drove her to Boise to the airport. A brooding, dark glare kept her quiet as he set her suitcase on the curb and pinned her with a final, departing glower.

The long drive back to Holiday gave him plenty of time to think of how he could have better handled the situation.

Definitely not allowing Hilary to kiss him, even if he had been trying to untangle himself from her clutches. That was when things went from bad to horrible.

The moment she'd stepped inside the house, he should have tossed her outside and locked the door.

The entire scene replayed over and over in his head. Shocked, he realized he hadn't even defended Fynlee when Hilary said those hateful things to her.

He was such an idiot. And a jerk. And a moron.

How had he ever let Hilary's appearance and false affection turn his head? Regret stabbed at him that he hadn't seen her real personality sooner. That he hadn't made certain she understood their relationship was over.

The look on Fynlee's face as she left made it clear she was devastated. She had every right to be.

But if he couldn't figure out a way to talk her into giving him another chance, he didn't know what he'd do.

A future without Fynlee in it didn't even bear consideration.

Chapter Ten

Tears didn't mar Fynlee's vision as she drove back to Golden Skies after leaving the Flying B. Dry-eyed and strangely detached from her emotions, she walked Ruth and her grandmother inside and accompanied them to Matilda's room.

The two women insisted she stay with them awhile although she really wanted to be alone.

Matilda made three cups of hot chocolate and set a plate of cookies on the coffee table before she and Ruth took seats on the couch, flanking Fynlee.

Silently, the women drank the chocolate and nibbled at the cookies.

Unable to endure the quiet any longer, Ruth placed her hand on Fynlee's back and gave it a comforting pat.

The simple touch released a dam in the poor girl's heart and opened the floodgate of tears.

The torrent raged for so long, the two older

women had no idea what to do. Distraught, they dabbed at their tears while offering comforting words and plenty of hugs.

Finally, the storm subsided and Fynlee released a long breath. "I'm so sorry," she sniffled, taking the fresh box of tissues her grandmother held out to her. "I just…" She hiccupped and wiped her nose.

"It's okay, honey." Matilda hugged her tightly. "No one expected that… that…" Ruth shot her a cautionary glance, "… home wrecker to show up."

Ruth patted Fynlee's leg. "I know it looked bad, but in Carson's defense, he told me weeks ago he was through with Hilary. All day today, he couldn't stop talking about you. I don't think he had any idea Hilary planned to arrive and I'm certain he had no idea about that ring she wore on her finger."

"That was a gaudy thing, wasn't it?" Matilda observed.

"My word, yes." Ruth nodded her head. "Why, I've never…"

"But he kissed her!" Fynlee exclaimed, unable to get the vision of Hilary wrapped around Carson out of her head.

"It appeared that way," Ruth reluctantly agreed. "Perhaps it wasn't what it seemed. We were standing behind her and all the way across the room. Maybe she was the one doing all the kissing. It's possible Carson wasn't enjoying it."

Matilda huffed. "He shouldn't have allowed that two-bit hussy to get close enough to kiss him. Or touch him. And he sure shouldn't have let her spout off such nastiness to my girl."

Fynlee's tears started again and Ruth shook her

head, glaring at Matilda. As they comforted the crying girl, a loud knock sounded at the door.

Matilda hurried to stare through the peephole. Like a mother hen protecting her chick, she opened the door just enough she could stick out her index finger and shake it accusingly in Carson's face.

"How dare you come here after that mess you created!" The volume of her voice caused doors up and down the hall to open and residents to peer out, curious about the noise.

"May I please come in and explain?" Carson asked, edging closer to the opening in the door. He could have easily pushed it open, but he wouldn't out of respect to Matilda, no matter how much he wanted to. "Is Fynlee here? I went by her apartment, but no lights were on and her car wasn't there."

"Where my granddaughter happens to be is none of your concern. You made it clear where your loyalty lies this evening, so you stay away from her and leave her alone."

Matilda started to shut the door, but Carson placed a hand on it.

"Please, Matilda? I just want to explain what happened. I know I'm an idiot, but what you three think happened isn't what really happened."

"What is it you assume we think happened?" Matilda's index finger jabbed him in the chest with each syllable she spoke.

Carson took a step back before her bony finger punctured his lung. "If I had to guess, I'd say you think I really did propose to Hilary, invited her to spend Christmas with me, and have been toying with Fynlee's affections as a welcome diversion to pass the time."

Matilda stepped back and Carson released a breath, expecting to be welcomed inside. Much to his dismay, his aunt took the other woman's position in blockading the door.

"Carson, not a single one of us wants to hear what you've got to say this evening. You've done enough damage. No matter what you might say, we all saw what happened when that… that… brazen strumpet arrived." Ruth pointed toward the elevator down the hall. "For tonight, it's best if you leave."

"I'm sorry, Aunt Ruth. I really didn't…"

With finality, the door shut in his face.

When Ruth and Matilda turned back around, Fynlee smiled through her tears at her two defenders and protectors. "Thank you. I just can't see him right now. I'm too…"

"Angry," Matilda said, taking a seat beside Fynlee on the couch.

"Disappointed," Ruth interjected, sitting on Fynlee's other side.

Once the two women finally went to bed, Fynlee curled up on the couch under one of Matilda's soft fleece blankets and wondered how she'd been so stupid. She'd known all along Carson was in love with Hilary and always would be.

The next morning, three sad women shared a solemn breakfast in Ruth's apartment. Since they'd taken all their gifts out to the Flying B the previous day in anticipation of opening them there before they shared Christmas dinner together, they didn't even have anything to open. However, there wasn't a gift in the world that would compel Fynlee to drive out to the Flying B to reclaim their packages.

After washing the breakfast dishes, Fynlee kissed the velvety cheeks of the two elderly women and returned to her apartment. Barely making it to her bed, she flopped down and cried for another hour before she forced herself to stop and take a shower.

Facts assailed her as she stood in the steamy water. Carson hadn't made her any promises. He'd never said a word about his feelings. For all she knew, the kisses he lavished on her last night could have come from a mixture of too many sugary treats and Christmas excitement.

Convinced her longing for him to love her had created something that didn't exist, she vowed to move beyond her shattered heart, the one Carson had glibly said he'd never break, and pull herself together. After all, it was Christmas Day, and she'd promised Ruth and Matilda she'd eat lunch with them.

When she returned to Golden Skies, a pile of packages surrounded the table in Ruth's apartment where she'd decorated a miniature artificial tree.

"Carson brought these in a while ago," Ruth said, wrapping an arm around Fynlee's waist as she stared at the brightly wrapped presents. "I told him I wouldn't open the door enough for him to leave them if he tried to say one word about what happened yesterday, so he carried them in and left."

Fynlee blinked back her tears. The thought that Ruth chose to spend the day with her rather than her own beloved nephew made her heart pinch with pain. Unless Hilary was still around, Carson would spend a long, lonely day.

The other two women didn't appear concerned about whether he had company or not, so they sat down and opened the packages.

Tears dripped down all their cheeks when they opened the gifts from Carson. In addition to Ruth's bouquet of carved flowers to hang on the wall, he'd also made Matilda a bright yellow sunflower clock.

Fynlee traced her finger over the perfect rose carved into the lid of the keepsake box Carson made for her. The attention to detail, the painstaking hours he'd spent on the gift, left her grabbing for Ruth's box of tissues.

Christmas turned into one of the most miserable days Fynlee could ever recall experiencing.

Relieved when it was finally over, she slogged through the week between Christmas and New Year's with a heavy heart. Out of desperation for a distraction, she'd even volunteered to work at the billing center. Regrettably, Carrie didn't need the additional help.

New Year's Eve found her sitting alone in her apartment at midnight, eating a pint of strawberry ice cream. The silly fantasies she'd harbored of ringing in the New Year at the Flying B, sharing a special midnight kiss with Carson, assailed her.

Recollections of how good it felt to be in his arms, wrapped in the warmth of his presence, made her heart hurt so badly, she set aside the ice cream and clutched a pillow to her chest.

Carson was everything she'd dreamed of

finding in a man. He was so good with her grandmother, so kind, patient, and giving. He was funny and light-hearted, and a hard worker. Then there was the matter of his handsome face and broad shoulders and…

Fynlee stopped before she made herself any more miserable. Her resolution for the New Year was to get over Carson and move on with her life.

The following Monday, she started her new job at Golden Skies. Although she had much to learn, she loved the work and was thrilled to be close to Matilda and Ruth.

They insisted on taking her out to dinner to celebrate making it through her first week of work.

As they sat together in a booth at the diner, Ruth gave Matilda a look and tipped her head toward Fynlee.

"Say, honey, Ruth had a chance to sit down and visit with Carson about what happened Christmas Eve. That boy couldn't be sorrier…"

Fynlee tossed down her napkin and stood to her feet. "I don't want to hear one word about Carson and what happened. Not a single one. I will walk out that door and leave you two to find your own way back to Golden Skies if you so much as even think about saying another word in his defense."

Matilda pulled on her hand until she sat back down in the booth, and wrapped an arm around her shoulders. "We won't say anything, sweetheart, but you really should listen to what he has to say."

"Grams, I mean it." Fynlee scooted toward the edge of the booth. "Not another word."

Ruth and Matilda nodded in agreement,

although it wouldn't be their last attempt at setting things right between Carson and Fynlee. Anyone could see the two of them were miserable and so utterly in love.

Carson had tried texting and calling Fynlee to apologize. He'd sent flowers that she'd thrown away without reading the card. She'd refused to sit near him at church, and shredded the letter he'd mailed her as a last-ditch effort at getting through to her.

At wit's end, he'd gone to his aunt and begged her to try to get Fynlee to see reason.

Ruth sighed. It appeared there would be no rationalizing with the broken-hearted girl.

Chapter Eleven

"This is just unacceptable, Tillie. We were so close to getting those two kids together then that... that... silicone-enhanced charlatan had to show up and ruin everything." Ruth took a sip of her tea then set down the cup with a clatter. The ever-present handkerchief she kept tucked in her pocket appeared and she dabbed at her eyes. "Once he explained everything, it made perfect sense. My heart just hurts for them both."

"Well, sitting here like a couple of whiny crybabies isn't going to fix this mess." Matilda leaned forward and studied her friend. A mischievous gleam glistened in her eyes behind her round glasses when she finally spoke. "If there was an emergency and you needed Carson to come immediately, how fast would he get here?"

Baffled by the question, Ruth stared at her. "As you well know, it usually takes about twenty minutes from the ranch to here. If he drove fast and the roads were clear, he could probably make it in fifteen. Why?"

"You better hold on to your girdle, Ruthie, because we're gonna burn this place to the ground so Carson and Fynlee will have to come to the rescue."

Ruth rose to her feet and grinned. "I haven't worn a girdle since 1987 but I've got a whole book of matches. Where do we start?"

"Are we ready to do this?" Matilda asked, glancing over her shoulder at Ruth and Rand Milton.

Unable to pull off their devious plans alone, Matilda had enlisted the assistance of any resident of Golden Skies willing to help, along with a few friends in town.

Ruth smiled at Rand. He grinned and pushed the button on a walkie-talkie. "Squadrons ready, over?"

A static response of "check" reverberated back to them.

"We're ready to rock and roll," Rand said. The look of eager anticipation on his face nearly matched that of the two matchmaking old women.

Matilda nodded. "Okay, Ruthie. You're on and you've got to make it convincing."

"I'll have you know I starred in the senior class play and received a standing ovation," Ruth said, picking up her cell phone and calling Carson.

The second time the phone rang, she nervously plucked at the sleeve of her dress. The third ring left her heart pounding in trepidation.

On the verge of hanging up, relief swept through her when he answered on the fourth ring.

"Hey, Aunt Ruth. I didn't forget about taking you to the grocery store tomorrow. I'll be there around nine…"

"Carson! You've got to come right away!" Ruth inflicted a great deal of panic into her voice.

"What's wrong? Are you hurt? Is everything okay?"

Ruth coughed a few times and added a hint of hysteria to her tone. "Oh, the flames! My gracious! Carson, please help me! Please!"

Rand crumpled a piece of paper against the phone and Ruth abruptly disconnected the call, pretending they'd been cut off.

"Set that timer," Ruth said, pointing to the egg timer next to Matilda. As soon as it was set, she pointed to her friend. "Now, you make sure Fynlee is on her way."

Matilda placed a hasty call to the sandwich shop where they'd sent Fynlee to bring back their noon meal. They told her they didn't feel like fixing lunch and nothing in the cafeteria sounded good. They claimed to have a craving for the special chicken and rice soup the deli made. Surprised by their request, Fynlee promised to return soon with soup and sandwiches for them all.

A grin stretched the corners of Matilda's orange lipstick-covered mouth upward as she hung up the phone and looked to her two cohorts in crime. "She was just checking out. By the time she gets to her car and drives back here, it should work perfectly."

"Just in case, we've got our backup contingency ready. Right?" Ruth asked Rand.

"Yes, ma'am, we do."

The three of them enjoyed a few sips of coffee before Matilda glanced at the sunflower clock on the wall, her Christmas gift from Carson, then the timer. "It's time to light a fire."

Five toasters sat in front of her living room window. They dropped bread in the slots and turned each toaster to the darkest setting. When the toast popped up, they pushed the buttons back down, waiting for the toast to burn.

Rand opened the window and lifted a blow dryer, fanning the smoke outside as the bread began to smolder. The smoke rolled out the window of Matilda's room.

Ruth insisted they let Sage and the rest of the staff in on their devious plans to keep from having the fire department show up for an unnecessary rescue. Although Matilda thought it would add to the authenticity of their scheme, Ruth and Rand outvoted her.

"We need more bread!" Ruth declared. She fished the burned toast onto a plate and dropped in more slices to turn into charred, blackened lumps.

"Oh, look, there's Carson!" Matilda pointed to a pickup wheeling into the parking lot. He left it near the curb and jumped out at a run.

"Quick, Rand. We need to slow him down until

Fynlee gets here." Ruth took the blow dryer from him while Rand grabbed his walkie-talkie.

"Squadron One, mount the elevator now! Squadron Two, take the stairs!"

"We're on it, sir!" A voice crackled back to them. Rand was practically dancing a jig as he looked back at Ruth and Matilda.

Matilda lifted a wooden yardstick with a bright red brassiere fastened to the end.

"Where on earth did you get that thing?" Ruth asked, staring at the undergarment of gigantic proportions.

"I borrowed it from Mrs. Freemont," Matilda said, waving the bra out the window with all the finesse of a flag-bearer in a parade, hoping to catch Fynlee's attention. "I didn't tell her what I wanted it for, though."

"Perhaps it would be best not to mention that detail when you return it," Ruth suggested. She glared at Rand as he stared at the bright red beacon, highlighted by the silvery-gray background of the January sky.

"Here she comes." Matilda grinned at Ruth then leaned out the window, coughing and fluttering her hand in feigned distress.

Carson had never been so scared in his life. Aunt Ruth sounded like she was about to die and her comment about flames sent him running out to his pickup without taking time to even grab his coat.

It was a good thing he still had on his boots from working outside that morning, or he would have raced through the snow in his socks.

The trip that usually took him twenty minutes into town passed in a shade past ten. He didn't even bother to park when he arrived at Golden Skies. Slamming on the brakes, he left the truck at the curb out front, noticing dark smoke coming from one of the resident's apartment windows. If he wasn't mistaken, it was Matilda Dale's room.

Long legs carried him through the lobby to the elevator in a matter of seconds. A frustrated yell threatened to work its way loose when he pushed the elevator button and a herd of residents in walkers and wheelchairs slowly exited. Impatient to reach his aunt, he raced down the hall to the stairs but found three residents blocking the door with their walkers, chatting about the latest issue of *AARP The Magazine*.

"Pardon me, please," he said, trying to work his way around them. Although he had to battle the urge to pick up the three women and carry them out of his way, he finally edged past them enough to open the stairwell door and slide inside. As he took the stairs two and three at a time, he hoped someone had already called 9-1-1.

At the third floor, he yanked open the door and nearly fell to his knees when a body shot off the elevator and slammed into him.

Fynlee smiled as she parked her car and started across the parking lot with a box from the deli. Gram and Ruth rarely asked her to bring them anything special, so she was more than happy to pick up the soup and sandwiches they'd requested.

Movement out of the corner of her eye caught her attention and she glanced up to see smoke billowing from Matilda's room.

A red bra waved in the frosty pearl-toned sky like a flag for help. Fynlee sucked in a frozen breath when her grandmother leaned out the window, gasping for air.

"Grams? Grams!" she screamed, dropping the box and sprinting across the parking lot. She flew past the receptionist's desk to the elevator and frantically pushed the button for the third floor.

The door wasn't fully open when she leaped off the elevator and smacked into Carson as he raced down the hall.

He grabbed her arms to keep her from falling and gave her a startled look. "Which one is it?" he asked.

"Grams. The smoke's coming from her place."

Together they hurried to Matilda's apartment, only to find the door open.

"Grams!" Fynlee scanned the living room then hurried into the bedroom. Carson checked in the kitchen. The sound of the front door slamming shut startled them both.

They hurried back into the living room. Carson tried the door but the knob fell off in his hand.

As he gazed from it to Fynlee, the lingering odor of burnt toast assaulted his senses. A look at the card table shoved beneath the window revealed a plate full of blackened bread and a row of toasters. A bright red bra of enormous magnitude tied to a wooden yardstick draped across the seat of a nearby chair.

Carson set the knob on an end table and walked over to the toasters. "I think we've been scammed."

"Are you kidding me?" Fynlee sank onto the couch and held a hand to her heart as it continued rapidly pounding in her chest. "They just scared ten years off my life. When I get my hands on Grams, she's gonna be in so much trouble."

"No more trouble than Aunt Ruth. She called me, pleading for me to rescue her then the line went dead. I broke at least a dozen traffic laws and used up eight lives of a cat crossing the road hustling to get here." Carson tossed the burnt toast out the window and closed it. The room was chilly from the winter air freely flowing into it. With the toast gone, the burnt smell quickly disappeared.

Carson picked up the yardstick and waved the eye-popping undergarment in Fynlee's direction. "What were they doing with this?"

A giggle burst out of Fynlee. She clapped a hand over her mouth, but the moment she looked at Carson, she couldn't hold back the laughter. He sank down on a canary yellow side chair and laughed until he had to wipe the moisture from his eyes.

"Those two old gals are going to be the death of me," he wheezed, trying to catch his breath.

Fynlee snatched tissues from a box near the couch and dabbed the tears from her eyes. "Get in line. They are going to kill me off first." She sighed and sank back against the colorful red and pink pillows on Gram's couch.

It was easy to be angry with Carson when she wasn't around him. Seated across from him as they attempted to recover from Ruth and Matilda frightening them so badly was an entirely different matter.

In spite of what happened, or didn't happen with Hilary, Carson was one of the most caring men she'd ever encountered.

A sigh of regret rolled out of her as she studied him, studied the rise and fall of his broad chest and the amusement lingering in the depths of his warm blue eyes. No matter how much she'd protested otherwise, she'd missed him, missed the easy friendship they shared.

No longer interested in holding onto her anger, she gave him a small smile. "I suppose if they went to this much effort to get us together, I should at least listen to whatever it is you've been trying to say to me since Christmas."

Bowled over by her unexpected willingness to hear him out, Carson took a moment to gather his wits.

"First, I want to apologize to you for what happened Christmas Eve. I had no idea Hilary planned to ambush me and I certainly had no inkling she thought I would marry her. And that kiss was all her, not me. Your grandmother and Ruth gave me exacting details how that might have appeared otherwise and you have to believe me, I didn't enjoy a second of it." Involuntarily, Carson's hand reached back and rubbed across the healing scabs on his neck.

Fynlee shot him a look full of doubt, but kept her mouth closed.

"As unbelievable as it may seem, in light of her words and actions that night, I broke up with Hilary when I went home for Thanksgiving. I thought she understood that I didn't want to see her again, but she has a hard time taking no for an answer. The ring she wore was one she picked out and her father purchased. There is absolutely no chance I'll marry her. Not ever." Carson leaned forward and braced his elbows on his knees. "I should have made sure she understood I meant it when I ended the relationship. It's one of those unpleasant things that I really didn't want to deal with, so I assumed she'd figure it out and hoped for the best."

Barely suppressing a disdainful sniff, Fynlee glared at him. "How'd that work out for you?"

"Not well," Carson sighed and sat back in the chair. "It not only ruined Christmas for me and three people I care about very much, it may have cost me the woman I love."

At Fynlee's surprised expression, he smiled at her. "I do love you, Fynlee. I've loved you since the day I stepped off the elevator with Aunt Ruth and you stood there holding an armful of your grandpa's old underwear. I wanted to tell you how I felt at the harvest party, but Hilary showed up and you know how that ended. I felt an obligation to her because we'd been together for so long. But the more time I spent with you, the more I realized there is only one person right for me. That person is you."

Although her eyes filled with tears and her frown softened into a smile, Fynlee remained silent.

"When Hilary showed up Christmas Eve, the whole thing caught me off guard. It's no secret that I handled the situation badly. I should have marched her to the door and tossed her out in the snow instead of letting her say all those spiteful things to you. I certainly shouldn't have allowed her to kiss me. In case I didn't sufficiently emphasize the point, she was doing the kissing, not me. As soon as I got my head on straight, I drove her to the airport in Boise and left her there, after making it crystal clear I never want to see her again."

Carson moved to the couch and sat next to Fynlee, taking her hand in his. The gentle, slow circles his thumb rubbed across her palm made any remaining remnants of her anger and indignation fall away.

"I never planned on marrying Hilary. Anytime I thought about marriage, something just didn't feel right. Now I know that's because she wasn't the one for me. You are."

"I am?" Fynlee stared at their joined hands, observing how right they looked together. How good they felt together.

"Yes, you are." Carson smiled at her with his heart in his eyes.

She swallowed hard as the last of her resistance melted.

"Every time I tried to envision a future with Hilary, all it did was give me indigestion. A lifetime of whining, nagging, driving her to nail appointments, and investing a small fortune in Miss

Clairol isn't what I want." Carson slid a little closer to her. "When I think of my future, I picture dark-haired kids with freckled noses running around the backyard. Long evenings spent watching sunsets from the porch. Afternoon rides along the fence line. Growing old and as crazy as Aunt Ruth and your grandmother — together. That's what I want, Fynlee. A future with you. There's nothing I'd like more than to spend every single day I have left on this earth showing you how much I love and cherish you. Can you somehow find a way to forgive me?"

Fynlee ignored the tears dripping down her cheeks and wrapped her arms around him, breathing in his familiar scent and absorbing his warmth into her soul. "Yes, I forgive you, if you can forgive me. I love you, Carson, and I'm sorry I've been so stubborn, refusing to see you. It's just that…"

When she hesitated, he pulled back and offered her an encouraging look. "Just what?"

"Hilary is beautiful and petite and so put together. It just didn't seem realistic that you'd be interested in a girl like me. I'm tall and goofy, with freckles and weird hair, and a loony grandmother and…"

Carson's kiss cut off anything else she might have said. Once he released her lips, he smiled at her with unbridled adoration.

"You're gorgeous, funny, smart, kind, and perfect for me, Fynlee Rose Dale. You've taught me about loving unselfishly, of what it means to truly care about others." He dropped down to one knee. "I don't have a ring, but you have my whole heart, Rosie Red, for as long as you want it. Will you please do me the honor of becoming my wife?" He offered her a charming grin. "If you say no, just think how disappointed all the participants in today's performance will be."

"I couldn't very well refuse and let them all down," Fynlee said, wrapping her arms around Carson's neck. "Yes, I'll marry you, but only if you promise we can have a Valentine's Day wedding. Christmas was awful and I spent New Year's Eve crying into my pillow. I want the next holiday to be one we'll always remember, one full of love and laughter. Besides, I seem to recall you teasing me about a Valentine's Day wedding the night we were snowed in at your place."

"You've got it, sweetheart. Since I plan to spend the next fifty or sixty years romancing you every single day, a Valentine's Day wedding sounds perfect." As their lips connected, he sat on the couch and pulled her onto his lap, pouring out his love with each kiss until everything else in the world faded from existence.

The sound of voices outside the door finally drew them back to reality. Hand in hand, they made their way over to the portal and peeked out. Fynlee clapped a hand over her mouth to keep from giggling at the sight of Matilda, Ruth and Rand holding glasses against the door, trying to listen.

Carson kissed her cheek then bent down so his mouth was close to the hole left by the missing doorknob. "She said yes, so if you want to join in our wedding plans, you better get us out of here."

"I'm on it!" Rand said while Ruth and Matilda squealed with excitement.

Carson and Fynlee both laughed at the crackle of the walkie-talkie as Rand called in more troops. "Squadron Six, get that doorknob repair kit up here ASAP!"

Chapter Twelve

Fat, fluffy snowflakes lazily drifted from the February sky as Carson watched his bride glide down the aisle on the arm of his father.

The red silk roses and cascade of crimson ribbon across the front of her white organza gown stood out against the snowy backdrop of the Golden Skies courtyard where they exchanged vows on Valentine's Day.

As his father placed Fynlee's hand on his arm and winked at him, Carson grinned.

Throughout the ceremony, he continued stealing glimpses of Fynlee, fighting the urge to pinch himself to make sure he was really marrying the entrancing girl who had completely stolen his heart.

When the pastor pronounced the couple man and wife, Carson lifted her filmy veil and tenderly took her face in his big hands, giving her a sweet gentle kiss that set every female heart in attendance aflutter.

After another dreamy kiss, they turned to face the guests at their wedding.

"I can't believe they pulled this off," Carson whispered to Fynlee, stirring the dark curls by her ear.

"Considering the fake fire they staged to get us together, I think this bunch can do anything they set their minds to." Fynlee leaned into Carson as he wrapped an arm around her against the chill in the air. "Everything is so beautiful."

"It really is," Carson agreed, reflecting on the past few weeks since he proposed to Fynlee.

Once Rand repaired the doorknob and freed them from Matilda's room, he and Fynlee announced their desire to wed on Valentine's Day.

Matilda and Ruth jumped into wedding plans with both feet, begging the couple to allow them to pull everything together.

Since Carson had no opinions on any of the trappings associated with weddings, and Fynlee cared more about her grandmother and Ruth having fun than what the wedding would be like, they gave the two women free rein.

With Matilda's flair for the dramatic and Ruth's elegant taste, the two of them worked well together. Ruth had insisted on involving Carson's mother in the plans through a flurry of phone calls and one hectic weekend visit. The result of their combined labors ended with a winter fairytale wedding that took place in the courtyard at Golden Skies.

After settling on red, cream, and pink as the wedding colors, the women enlisted the help of all the residents who participated in the scheme to bring Carson and Fynlee together. In a few short weeks, they fashioned a plethora of Valentine-themed decorations as well as baking and decorating gorgeous heart-shaped cookies as wedding favors. White lights, tulle draping, and colorful red, white, cream, and pink quilts added to the romantic atmosphere at the ceremony.

From the bouquets Fynlee's attendants carried to the boutonnieres worn by the wedding party, the Golden Skies residents had put their best efforts into creating a dream wedding.

Every one of the residents who was able to be outside sat beneath the quilts on white-draped folding chairs, witnessing the vows Carson and Fynlee exchanged. Those who couldn't brave the cold watched out the windows with their noses pressed against the frosty glass, eager to observe every detail of the event. Carson's family sat in the front row with Ruth while Fynlee's friends huddled around Matilda.

Rather than precede their guests inside, the couple watched as people scurried into Golden Skies out of the cold.

Fynlee smiled at her grandmother, dressed from head to toe in bright red, as she hugged Ruth, clad in pale pink from her coat to her shoes. They led the way to the center's large activity room for the reception.

"There won't ever be a dull moment with those two schemers around," Carson said as his lips brushed near Fynlee's ear.

She gazed at him with a soft light in her eyes. "I certainly hope they keep us hopping for a good long while to come."

He took her hand in his, rubbing his thumb across her palm and over her wrist. "Me, too, Rosie Red. Happy Valentine's Day and happy wedding day to you."

"Thank you for making today so special, and for my roses," Fynlee said, kissing his cheek then glancing down at her bouquet.

As a surprise, Carson had carved Fynlee's wedding bouquet. The red and cream roses appeared so real, they could have easily been mistaken for hothouse blooms. Painstakingly, he'd individually carved each flower and the roses didn't weigh any more than one made of silk or fresh blossoms. Unlike real flowers that would wilt, the bouquet provided a lasting keepsake that meant the world to his cherished bride.

Fynlee studied her husband as they stepped inside. He wore a new black Stetson, a black cutaway tuxedo and his best pair of boots, polished to a high shine. She'd never seen him look more dashing and handsome.

And every inch of the wonderful six-foot-four man, with those broad shoulders and beguiling eyes, belonged to her. She leaned against him again and placed a kiss on his strong jaw. "Do you suppose they'd notice if we left for our honeymoon a little earlier than planned."

Carson swung her into his arms and kissed her with unrestrained urgency. "I'm willing to chance it if you are."

Before they could sneak away, Matilda and Ruth ushered them into the waiting crowd of guests.

The activity room glowed with more white lights, tulle, and Valentine's decorations. Fynlee couldn't imagine a professional wedding planner fashioning anything more lovely than the wedding her loved ones had given her.

Carson started to lead her across the room when his mother intercepted them, giving them both warm hugs.

"If I haven't mentioned it before, I'm so, so happy to welcome you to our family, Fynlee. You're such a lovely girl and absolutely perfect for my rascally son." Evie Ford squeezed Fynlee's hand as she spoke.

Carson snorted. "You've mentioned it about a million times, Mom, but I'm glad my beautiful bride received your stamp of approval."

Evie smacked his arm. "Fynlee isn't just beautiful, Carson, she's smart and sweet and the best thing that has ever happened to you."

"Yes, ma'am, she is." Carson winked at his bride as his mother rushed off to discuss something with Ruth and Matilda.

"In case you haven't figured it out yet, my mom likes you." Carson whispered in Fynlee's ear as he walked her across the room to the table where they were supposed to sit.

"I thought perhaps she might, at least a little," Fynlee grinned. "The feeling is entirely mutual. How could I not love her? She's so friendly and fun. I'm glad Grams and Aunt Ruth included her in the wedding plans."

Carson held out her chair then took a seat beside her once she settled her full skirts. "You've set a challenging standard for my poor brothers, though."

The puzzled look she gave him made him laugh. "After this," Carson waved his hand around the room, "Mom will expect their brides to allow her to be bossy at their weddings, too. No wonder you'll be the favorite daughter-in-law."

Fynlee rolled her eyes although she grinned. "Maybe your brothers will show you and I'll be the only daughter-in-law."

Carson raised an eyebrow and tipped his head in the direction of his brothers. One of them appeared involved in a conversation with Fynlee's friend Carrie while another cast interested glances at Sage as she helped the Golden Skies residents find seats at tables.

After a meal catered by the kitchen staff at Golden Skies, the band that played at the harvest party took to the stage.

Fynlee and Carson enjoyed watching their family and friends throughout the afternoon.

When Rand waltzed by with Ruth in his arms, Fynlee gave Carson a knowing look. The older couple had danced together several times, much to her amusement.

Not one to be left out of the fun, Matilda spent plenty of time on the dance floor. Fynlee grinned when she twirled by on the arm of Carson's oldest brother.

"Your brothers have been absolutely

wonderful. I appreciate them being so nice to Grams."

"They think she's a hoot, like the rest of us." Carson kissed her tenderly with a hint of passion as they danced. "I love you so much, Fynlee. Thank you for marrying me."

"I love you, too, my hunky husband." Fynlee's gaze held golden sparks that ignited flames in Carson's blue eyes. "Thank you for giving me your heart and making me your forever Valentine. You have no idea how many dreams I dreamed of you, of loving you."

"I do have an idea because I was dreaming the same dreams of you, my beautiful, beloved Valentine Bride." He drew her closer to his heart and kissed her with the promise of a lifetime of love.

The Beginning...

Keep reading for a preview of the next Holiday Brides story!

Parmesan Fries

A friend and I ate dinner at a trendy restaurant where we indulged in an order of fries.

They weren't just any fries, though. They were crispy yet soft with a decadent Parmesan coating accented with fresh parsley.

After searching online for a recipe, I found this simple one. For an added flavor boost, toss the fries with a dash of truffle oil before serving.

Parmesan Fries
4 large unpeeled potatoes
1/4 cup olive oil
1/2 teaspoon salt
1 teaspoon powdered ranch seasoning
3/4 cup grated Parmesan cheese, divided
1/4 cup chopped fresh parsley
1 teaspoon truffle oil (optional)

Preheat an oven to 425 degrees F.

Wash the potatoes and cut into wedges (russets work best). Place the potatoes in a mixing bowl (or a resealable bag) and drizzle with olive oil. Sprinkle with salt and ranch seasoning. Toss until evenly coated. Spread the fries onto a nonstick baking sheet in a single layer.

Bake 30 minutes, flipping the fries halfway through baking.

Return the fries to the bowl (or the bag). Sprinkle with 1/2 cup Parmesan cheese and parsley. (If you want to add the truffle oil, do that at this point in the process). Toss to coat, and then spread again onto the baking sheet. Return to the oven, and bake until the Parmesan cheese melts, about 10 minutes. Sprinkle the fries with the remaining 1/4 cup Parmesan cheese and a dash of salt then serve.

Makes approximately four servings.

Author's Note

Sometimes the ideas for stories begin in the most unlikely places. A few years ago, my cousin shared a hilarious story about an elderly woman who'd taken to wearing her husband's underwear, because it provided such a wonderful lipstick holder.

Every time I thought about her logic, I'd get the giggles. Then my overactive imagination jumped in.

What if the woman wasn't in the beginning stages of dementia, but just a little kooky? What if she had a single granddaughter in need of a good man? What if she lived in a retirement village and kept the residents there on their toes?

That's when Matilda was born.

As a young girl, I heard my aunt and her friend laugh about that poem *"When I Am An Old Woman,"* by Jenny Joseph. They vowed to one day wear purple (and gold lamé) along with red hats, and to be indescribably outrageous when they were old enough to shock people and not care what anyone thought.

To date, my aunt hasn't worn purple or gold lamé or a red hat, but I've always admired the idea of being a person who wears what they please and does what they want without giving a thought to what others might think.

Matilda is just that kind of person. Is she wacky? Absolutely. But she's also kind and fun, and completely devoted to her granddaughter.

When I was developing her character, I knew Matilda needed a sidekick. Someone completely different from her charge-ahead personality. Don't ask me why, but the mother of one of my former classmates came to mind. Her name was Ruth and I always thought she looked like such a beautiful well-dressed lady, and she had such an air of poise and grace. I think there were eight kids in the family, so I'm sure she had her moments of keeping up with her children, but she had the softest, most pleasant voice and manner. So, my inspiration for Ruth derives from a real-life person.

I was supposed to be writing a Christmas story when the idea for a Valentine bride kept poking at me. The characters of Fynlee and Carson were relentless and I finally surrendered to their insistence that I tell their story.

In fact, I had such fun writing the story, I decided we need to revisit the residents of Golden Skies in future stories, so watch for more novellas set in the fictional town of Holiday with Matilda, Ruth, the dandy Rand Milton, Carson and Fynlee.

Oh, if you'd like to know the salve Carson purchased for Fynlee when she had saddle sores, it's Bag Balm. If you've never heard of it, run down to your local feed store or pharmacy and pick up a tin. It is wonderful stuff!

As always, thank you for reading the stories I write!

Thank You

Thank you for reading ***Valentine Bride.*** I hope you enjoyed the story leading to Fynlee and Carson's happily ever after. If you did, I'd be so appreciative if you'd consider leaving a review so other readers might discover the book, too.

If you liked reading about the town of Holiday, be sure to check out all of the Holiday Brides books!

Holiday Express
Four generations discover the wonder of falling in love and the magic of one very special train in these sweet romances.

Also, if you haven't yet signed up for my newsletter, won't you consider subscribing? I send it out when I have new releases, sales, or news of freebies to share. Each month, you can enter an exclusive giveaway, get a new recipe to try, and discover details about upcoming events. When you sign up, you'll receive a free digital book. Don't wait. Sign up today!

And if newsletters aren't your thing, please follow me on BookBub. You'll receive notifications on pre-orders, new releases, and sale books!

Will their mischief lead to love?

Sage Presley loves her job as the receptionist at Golden Skies Retirement Village in Holiday, Oregon. She enjoys the residents and their wisdom, even if some of them are more than a little quirky. Determined to ignore the matchmaking efforts of two women at the retirement home, Sage's sole focus is on raising her brother, Shane. In spite of her best efforts, she can't help but notice the hunky electrician who continually comes to her rescue.

Grateful for the opportunity to open his own electrical business, Justin James moves to Holiday full of plans and dreams. He's quickly drawn in by the close-knit community, but finds the lack of suitable single women disturbing. Despite himself, his attention is captured by the receptionist at the retirement home where he's working on a big job. Yet, he can't begin to understand why two matchmaking octogenarians are intent on forcing him together with the woman he's convinced is married.

A sweet romance sprinkled with humor, hope, and the meaning of real love, *Summer Bride* will warm the hearts of readers while bringing them a smile.

Preview Summer Bride

"What's a guy got to do to get a girl in this town?"

The men around Justin James stopped working and burst into uncontrollable laughter.

Shocked by their reaction to his query, he looked up from the conduit he was in the midst of bending and glared at the construction crew. As the electrician hired for Golden Skies Retirement Village's new wing and therapy center, he'd spent the last two weeks around the crew working on the project. Until that moment, he'd considered them friends. Now they approached enemy status.

"You ever thought about getting a little work done?" one of the men asked in a mocking tone. "If you try being someone other than yourself, maybe it would help."

"Yeah, you might want to step up your game, like taking a shower once in a while," another joked.

Those who hadn't already left for the day chuckled and guffawed, stirring Justin's temper. Under normal circumstances, Justin was easy-going and affable. But the ongoing hilarity about a problem he wanted addressed was about to wear his patience dangerously thin.

"What's so funny?" he asked, drawing more amusement at his expense. The men looked like dusty bobble-headed bozos as they doubled over with mirth, hardhats nearly crashing together as they wheezed and chortled.

"I don't have a problem finding girls around here," a man named Joe said when he finally stopped laughing.

A stocky construction guy named Tim snorted and pointed at Joe. "You find them, Joe, but it's keeping them where you run into trouble. Didn't you just finalize your divorce from wife number four?"

"Three, but who's counting," Joe said, glaring at Tim. He turned his attention back to Justin. "Maybe you should lower your standards."

Not that Justin had exceptionally high expectations to begin with, but his catalog of requirements was reasonable for a woman to be considered dating material. His checklist was simple: clean, groomed, IQ higher than dirt, self-efficient, nice, friendly, and a sense of humor. He counted it as a bonus if the woman was attractive, gainfully employed, and possessed good manners.

"My standards are just fine," Justin said defensively. He wished he'd never voiced the thoughts that had been running through his head as they finished up their work for the evening.

One of the first things he'd noticed when he'd moved to the small Eastern Oregon town of Holiday a week before Thanksgiving was the lack of eligible females.

"There are lots of unmarried women here at Golden Skies," Tim said, causing another round of laughter.

Widowed women ranging in age from seventy to nearly one hundred resided at the retirement village. They were definitely not dating material. He had enough trouble keeping the old women at bay as it was.

A few times he'd been in the lobby waiting to speak to the director of Golden Skies when he was nearly accosted by one of the residents. A woman named Matilda Dale seemed to think it was her job to squeeze his biceps and bat her eyes at him. The flamboyant outfits she wore combined with her round black-framed glasses made her look like Harry Potter's demented granny. From the stories he heard, she was as wacky as her appearance indicated.

"Maybe you should try dating your own species. I heard they have an abundance of dogs at the rescue kennel in town," Joe deadpanned.

Justin knew the guys were trying to be funny, but their teasing irritated him. Normally, he would have joined in their jollity, but right now he wanted to give Joe a black eye. Or two.

Finally, one of the men noticed the somber expression on Justin's face and curtailed his amusement.

"Boss, are you serious?" asked Matt Smith, Justin's apprentice electrician and friend.

"Dead serious." Justin glanced over the group of men again before he returned his attention to the conduit. "Just forget I asked."

"No, dude." A man everyone called Bull thumped Justin on the shoulder, nearly toppling him to the floor.

Although he was six-feet tall in his sock-feet, Justin had to look up to Bull. He assumed the man's nickname derived from his massive size and not the fact he often told wild tales no one believed, but enjoyed all the same.

"It's a fair question," Bull said, looking at the others with a warning glare.

The men quieted and glanced at Justin again.

He shrugged. "In the few months I've lived here, I've gone out on exactly three disastrous dates. One gal conveniently forgot to mention she was married until her husband showed up at the pizza place and threatened to shoot us both. The second woman I took out never stopped talking the entire time I was stuck with her. She got shushed so many times at the movie theater, it's a wonder they didn't ask us to leave. I thought my ears might start bleeding before I called it a night. And the third was a doozy. The woman should be committed to a psycho ward, and I'm not joking. By the time we finished dinner, she was already talking about moving in with me and had picked out names for the three children she decided we'd have. When she demanded we drive to my place so she could analyze the demonic forces of the house, I couldn't get away from her fast enough."

A few chuckles rolled out of the men, but they gave Justin sympathetic looks.

"We've all been there, man," Bull said, and thumped him on the shoulder again. "Don't give up yet. There are some good women in town, too. Have you tried hanging out at The Blue?"

Justin shook his head. "The bar scene isn't really my thing, but thanks for sharing that tip, Bull."

The man nodded his head and looked to the others as they gathered their tools. "What about the grocery store? Women are always there."

"I tried picking up a girl there once," Tim said, grinning at the group. "I bumped into her cart on purpose to get her attention. I broke a dozen eggs and bruised her bananas. By the time she got done verbally dressing me down, I decided I didn't need a date that bad."

"How about the gas station?" Joe asked, yanking off his gloves and stuffing them in his back pocket. "You could be a hero and wash a windshield or two while the attendant pumps their gas."

With great effort, Justin refrained from rolling his eyes. "No, thanks. I don't have time for that, anyway."

"You could always join the PTA and hang out at the meetings. There are oodles of women there," Tim said with a mocking grin.

"Man, are you nuts?" Matt asked. "Most of the women attending meetings at the school are married. The ones who aren't are like wild animals attacking fresh meat when a single guy shows up."

"Don't forget if they are there, they've most likely got a kid or two, or six," Bull added.

Justin swallowed down an exasperated sigh. "Thanks for all that awesome advice," he said in a voice heavy with sarcasm. "Isn't it time for you jokers to leave for the day?"

"Yeah, it is," Bull said, gathering his things along with the rest of the crew. "Don't work too late."

"I won't. See you guys tomorrow." Justin waved at them as they left.

"Want me to help you with that conduit?" Matt asked as he prepared to leave.

"No. I'm just gonna finish this one piece and then I'll call it a night. Enjoy your evening, Matt."

"I will, boss," Matt said, picking up his lunch box and giving Justin a studying look. "Are you really trying to find a girl?"

Justin refused to say anything further on the subject after the guys offered so many unhelpful suggestions. "Nah, it's all good."

"If you really want to meet someone, my sister has a friend who just moved back to town. She's divorced, but no kids."

Justin glanced over his shoulder at Matt and tossed him a grin. "Maybe you should take her out, then."

Matt laughed. "Maybe I will. See you in the morning."

Justin finished with the piece of conduit then gathered his tools, pulled on his coat, and made sure everything was secured before he left for the evening.

As he walked through the cold drizzle of rain to his pickup, he thought about what the guys had said. He might not be the most handsome guy in the world, but Justin knew he was reasonably good looking. In spite of what was mentioned about him stepping up his game and attending to personal hygiene, Justin knew the guys were only joking. Of them all, he was the most well-groomed, at least most of the time.

His hand brushed over the stubble on his jaw and he tried to remember when he had last shaved. Maybe it was Monday? Or was it Sunday? It didn't really matter since he wouldn't be kissing anyone that night — or any night in the foreseeable future.

Until he moved to Holiday, he'd never had trouble getting a date, so he didn't think it was his personality.

He certainly wouldn't consider lowering his standards. After all, slightly dipping them had been the reason for the three horrible dates he'd endured.

Justin unlocked his pickup, set his tool bag on the backseat, and then climbed behind the wheel. He started the truck and let it warm up a minute to chase away the late February chill before he made his way home.

The one woman in town who had captured his interest turned out to be married. In fact, she worked right there at Golden Skies as the front desk receptionist. He'd seen Sage Presley around town a few times and had wondered about her, then the first time he set foot in the retirement village she'd greeted him with a warm, friendly smile.

Sage was everything he was looking for in a woman. She was sweet with the most intriguing green eyes. Her golden hair was thick and curly. Flawless skin and an amazing figure appeared model-worthy. And her beauty seemed to be far deeper than the surface. He'd seen her patiently and lovingly provide assistance to the residents of Golden Skies.

Eager to seize the opportunity to ask her out, he happened to notice a silver band on her ring finger before he blurted out a request to take her on a date. Then, much to his surprise, he'd watched her hug a boy who had to be entering his teen years and ask him if he was ready to go home. Justin overheard her inquiring about homework and how his day at school had been.

Either Sage had incredible genes that made her look far younger than her years, or she'd had a son at an unbelievably young age. If he had to guess, he would have pegged her as being in her early to mid-twenties.

She had to be older, though, especially with a boy that big. Since Justin was almost twenty-eight, he didn't mind a woman being a little older, although he wasn't sure he wanted to get involved with someone who had a child. Being a parent to a teen wasn't something he'd considered. Then again, Sage was already taken so it was a moot point.

Justin didn't know what it was, but he was tired of playing the field, tired of trying to figure out the ever-changing rules to the games people played while dating. He just wanted to find someone special to share his life with. Someone who made him look forward to coming home every night. Someone he could wrap his arms around and love with all his heart.

Determined to change the direction of his thoughts, Justin pulled out of the parking lot and decided to run by the grocery store on his way home. Who knew? Maybe he'd bump into a woman there, although he had no intention of stooping to underhanded tactics like cart crashing just to meet a girl.

Humor restored, he chuckled as he recalled the conversation he'd just had with the guys. Joining the PTA? He absolutely was not that desperate.

At least not yet.

Order *Summer Bride* today!
Available on Amazon!

More Sweet Romances by Shanna Hatfield

If you love reading about quirky small towns that would make the perfect Hallmark movie, check out the *Summer Creek Series*.

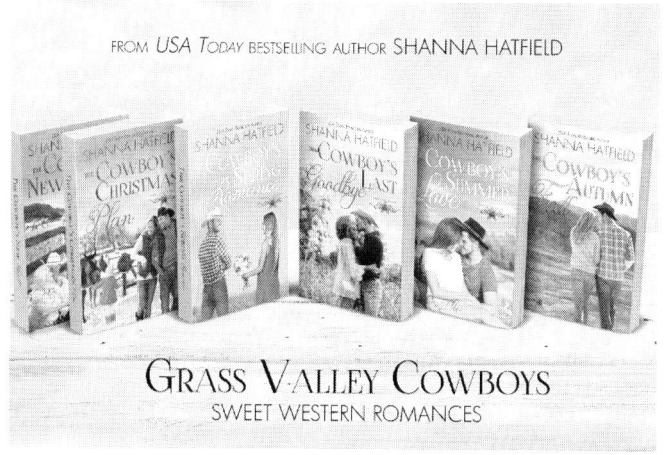

Fall in love with the Thompson brothers and their friends in the Grass Valley Cowboys series!

About the Author

PHOTO BY SHANA BAILEY PHOTOGRAPHY

USA Today bestselling author Shanna Hatfield is a farm girl who loves to write. Her sweet historical and contemporary romances are filled with sarcasm, humor, hope, and hunky heroes.

When Shanna isn't dreaming up unforgettable characters, twisting plots, or covertly seeking dark, decadent chocolate, she hangs out with her beloved husband, Captain Cavedweller, at their home in the Pacific Northwest.

Shanna loves to hear from readers. Connect with her online:

Blog: shannahatfield.com
Facebook: Shanna Hatfield's Page
Shanna Hatfield's Hopeless Romantics Group
Pinterest: Shanna Hatfield
Email: shanna@shannahatfield.com

Manufactured by Amazon.ca
Acheson, AB